DIARY OF AN 8-BIT WARRIOR

PATH OF THE DIAMOND

Published in French under the title *Journal d'un Noob (Vrai Guerrier) Tome IV*
© 2016 by 404 éditions, an imprint of Édi8, Paris, France
Text © 2015 by Cube Kid, Illustration © 2016 by Saboten

Minecraft is a Notch Development AB registered trademark. This book is a work of fiction and not an official Minecraft product, nor approved by or associated with Mojang. The other names, characters, places, and plots are either imagined by the author or used fictitiously.

Andrews McMeel Publishing
a division of Andrews McMeel Universal
1130 Walnut Street, Kansas City, Missouri 64106
www.andrewsmcmeel.com

17 18 19 20 21 RR2 10 9 8 7 6 5 4 3 2 1

ISBN: 978-1-4494-8009-7

Library of Congress Control Number: 2016934684

Made by:
RR Donnelley Printing Company Ltd.
Address and location of manufacturer:
1009 Sloan Street
Crawfordsville, IN 47933
1st printing—2/17/17

ATTENTION: SCHOOLS AND BUSINESSES
Andrews McMeel books are available at quantity discounts with bulk purchase for educational, business, or sales promotional use. For information, please e-mail the Andrews McMeel Publishing Special Sales Department: specialsales@amuniversal.com.

• CUBE KID •

DIARY OF AN 8-BIT WARRIOR

PATH OF THE DIAMOND

Illustrations by Saboten

Andrews McMeel
PUBLISHING®

In memory of Lola Salines (1986–2015),
founder of 404 éditions and editor of this series,
who lost her life in the November 2015 attacks on Paris.
Thank you for believing in me.

—Cube Kid

Here's Volume 4 !!!

If you haven't read the others, **you'll be like**

or even

0_0

I also **made this** for you:

it's a happy chicken.

My mind was a **water block** in the Nether. One second it was there, and then, with just a little puff of smoke, gone—*poof*—a **little wisp.**

First of all, the five best students would become **captains**, meaning they'd have their own squad to command. As if that wasn't **crazy enough**, Drill admitted that we might someday actually . . . **attack** . . . Herobrine's castle . . . how could we?!

I just don't get it!

Everyone around me was equally **flabbergasted**. Silence grew into murmurs, panicked voices, and questions, questions—**a whole lot of questions.** The most common question being: *"Mayor, sir, is it really true?"*

Alone up on the platform, the mayor **sighed again.** "Yes, it's true. It's something we've been considering, anyway. Now, if you'll all just **quiet down** . . ."

But they didn't quiet down.
Not at all. It was madness.
Madness. Total chaos.

Everyone was **shouting** at once, swarming the platform, asking the mayor an endless stream of questions.

Then an old man got so angry he looked to the sky and started **screaming at the top of his lungs.** *(I have no idea what his problem was.)*

Emerald **said it better** than I ever could *(although I could barely hear her over the constant roar):* "Um, did I hear that right? Not to rain on anyone's **enderman party** here, but, um, this is the **worst** news yet! Clearly Drill was talking about a different Herobrine. I mean, let's face it. There's no way he meant the Herobrine who sends out **streams of lightning** like a dispenser firing arrows, **turns people into rabbits** with the snap of his fingers, and, oh, **has entire legions** of super-powerful mobs under his control."

"**Yeah,** they can't be serious about attacking," Max said. "Knowing Herobrine, his castle probably doesn't even have gates or an entrance of any kind. Come to think of it, do they even know where his castle is located? I've found nothing on this, even after days and days of research." He nudged me. "Speaking of which, are you ready to **help me crack the books** tomorrow, buddy boy?"

Breeze commented with as few words as possible, as usual: "It's like my home village all over again."

Weirdly, Stump seemed a bit happy about this news. "This means I can slack off now! I don't care if I'm a captain, as long as I'm **crushing zombies** with you!"

Kolbert, too, was rather upbeat. "You villagers don't need captains!" He boomed. "**Path of the Diamond?** How about **Path of the Slain Zombies?** For that is what I, Kolbert of **Terraria,** will leave behind on my way to Herobrine's castle!"

A couple other humans looked at him strangely. "**Terraria?**"

He shrugged. "**What?** That's what these people call Earth. **Noobs.**"

(He was telling the truth. I only use "Earth" because I learned that word from Steve.)

Another thing to consider: **What if I somehow fail to become a captain?** If that happens, well . . . knowing my luck, I'd be placed under **Pebble's command.** I'd have to do whatever he tells me to do. I can only imagine how well that might turn out.

"Don't sulk! Carrying lava buckets is super important. You never know when the zombies could attack again, right? Hey! Let's not spill it everywhere, okay?"

If I thought my life at school was bad . . .
FAREWELL . . .

As the crowd grew louder and louder, pressing the mayor for answers, **something happened that nobody expected.** Steve appeared, with Mike at his side. That wasn't so strange in itself, but . . . **they were riding horses.**

I hadn't talked to them in a few days. Last I'd heard, they'd been **working overtime** on redstone contraptions. The sight of those two, as they approached the mayor's platform riding saddled mounts, caused the crowd to quiet down.

"If I may say one thing," Steve said. "Perhaps you should send **messengers** to the other villages. If you really are planning an attack in the future, you'll need all the help you can get."

The mayor nodded, gaze lowered, seemingly deep in thought, **then nodded again.** "An **excellent plan,** to be sure. But we must assume that Herobrine's forces are everywhere. Such a long journey would be **exceedingly dangerous,** even on horseback."

"Don't worry about us," Mike said. "It's not like we've ever failed you before."

Again, the mayor nodded. "**Indeed,** and I suspect you **never will. Very well.** Shall I send a guide to accompany you?"

"We'll manage," Steve said, and held up a **map and compass**.
"Count on it."

Steve was like **my mentor** and **big brother** at the same time.
Now he was leaving. Maybe he found this existence **too depressing** and
had to try to get away. However, when he rode over to me, I saw only
hope in his shiny, square eyes.

"I don't know what's happening, Runt. Every day I wake up hoping
to find that this is all a dream, just like Herobrine said. **But I know
it's not.** We're here for a reason. **I've got to help out.**"

"**But the village needs you!**" I said. "You humans are much more
creative than us."

He shook his head. "You may not see it, but you're **just as good** as
we are when it comes to defending this place."

"Hurrrm . . ."

"Plus, there's **another reason** why we're going," Mike said. "They
might have more **knowledge about crafting.** We'll try to bring back
some new toys."

"**Toys?** You mean **new items?** You'll give me one, right?"

"Well, yeah, um . . . sure. Of course."

"**Promise?**"

"**Super promise.**"

"Hurrr. Okay. **Deal.**"

With that, my **otherworldly friends** took off. They were the ones who had shown us that the mobs could be fought. Without them, we would have suffered the **same fate** as so many other villages out there. I imagined the endless wilderness outside of our walls. Plains and forests and rolling hills as far as the eye can see. **Littered** with the remnants of our kind. They'll be traveling through that for a long time. **Whatever.** That's their decision. Two months ago, I would have dwelt on it, gotten angry and sad. But I'm a new me now. **A future captain,** hopefully. I can't be whining and raging all the time. They can go on their little adventure. Meanwhile, **Team Runt** will be relaxing in the coolest place in Villagetown.

Party at the pool.

SPLASH!!!

For the first time in her life,
Breeze was beginning to **have fun.**

After the celebration, we went to **the pool.** The mobs wouldn't be coming back anytime soon, and we totally **needed a break.** The builders made this area **underground.** It used to be a giant cavern the miners had cleared out. The main attraction is the **heated water.** There's a small lava pool bubbling underneath the floor that heats it perpetually. From what the humans have told me, the game version of our world doesn't simulate temperature beyond melting snow and ice. **The real world isn't so forgiving.** Try spending a night in a **tundra biome.** You'll be throwing down a furnace real quick.

We changed into our swimming suits and **jumped in.** We agreed to play **Creeper's Revenge,** one of our favorite games. It's where a single "cat" must avoid the splashes of the many "creepers" as they dive in, over and over. You're probably wondering how we decide teams. After someone shouts "Go," the last one to call out "Boom" is the first to be the cat.

"Go!!"

"Boom."

"Boom!"

"Boom!!"

Breeze glanced at the three of us. "Boom?" *(She'd obviously never played this before.)* We all turned to Emerald.

"Looks like **you're the cat**," Stump said.

However, Emerald didn't respond. She was still standing on the edge of the shallow side, staring **absently** into the water.

So an enderman from the start?
I knew it!

So Breeze was happy and Emerald was sad. **What next?!** At this rate, Herobrine will teleport into our village and give everyone **milk and cookies**. I swam over to her. "Something bothering you?"

"Yeah. Me." She sat down and dipped her legs into the water. "I've been thinking, and . . . I just can't forgive myself."

"For what?"

"For running away. This is the second time I've chickened out." The other three swam over as well.

"Everyone ran yesterday," Breeze said. "Myself included. Don't blame yourself."

"Yeah, but you went back." Emerald exhaled, blowing her bangs upward. "It's funny, y'know? A lot of kids at school look up to me. They think I'm so brave."

I climbed up and sat down next to her. "This reminds me of something. During the second battle, with those zombies . . . why did you run?"

"Um, I was scared?"

"You came back with iron golems, didn't you?"

"Too little, too late."

"But you did the right thing. The same can be said for when you ran from Urkk. You went to go get the others. Even set off the fireworks Drill gave you."

The war heroine looked away. "So I follow orders. Great. What's your point?"

"I'll be the first one to say it," I said, glancing at everyone. "I've been awfully lucky. When Urkk chased me, what would have happened if

10

that **mushroom** hadn't been there? What would I have done? Or what if those skeletons had surrounded me yesterday?"

A slight grin broke out across Max's face. "I see what you're saying. **Good warriors** should know when to run."

I noddded. "**Exactly.** I can't keep being so reckless. My luck will run out eventually. If anything, Emerald, you can teach me a thing or two."

Breeze smirked. "**I hope she does.** Then maybe you'll rescue me someday."

Thankfully, my words seemed to help bring Emerald back to her normal, chipper self. "I did do pretty well during that first battle, huh? I didn't even have good items then! Sara thought she did better, but she had that **enchanted bow!** Just imagine how well I'll do once I have all the best stuff. **Hurmmph!**"

Stump let out a huge sigh. "Guys, why are we talking about this stuff? We're supposed to be **re-lax-ing,** remember? Let's play **Squid War!! Go!!**"

". . ."
". . ."
". . ."
". . ."

"Bloop?"
"What . . . ?"
"Uh, isn't that the sound **a squid makes?**"

Seriously?

"I've never played this game before, okay?"

"Never seen a squid before, either, apparently. Squids don't go **bloop!!**"

(Squids don't make noise at all, so the first person to say something gets to be the squid—in this case, Emerald.)

She flashed a huge grin. "So kind of you guys. Really."

(By the way, in this game, you really want to be the squid.)

SATURDAY NIGHT— UPDATE I

After the pool party, we went **shopping.** Although I didn't find any good swords, I traded for a book with **Respiration III** and **enchanted my hood.** *(It was on sale. It's not like anyone in this village has time for ocean diving.)* The next time Pebble tries to well-dunk me, he's going to be in for quite a surprise! **I'll just swim to the bottom and read a book!**

I walked Breeze back to her house just before the sun went down.

"**It's been really fun,**" she said.

"It was even better before the war," I said. "Wish you could've seen the town back then."

"**Yeah. Me, too.** Hey, let's go shopping again, huh?"

She lingered for a moment, until her father came out.

"**See you Monday,**" Brio said. "We've got some new classes. **You'll love them.**"

"What classes?" I asked.

He smirked. "**Wait and see.**"

With a smile, I nodded, **waved,** and shared a good-bye with Breeze—then I took off **under the stars.** The streets weren't entirely empty. These days, they **aren't exactly safe.** Even in the daytime. Even so close to the village center. After the sun goes down, you won't find anyone around. Just closed iron doors and windows with **iron bars.**

13

Yet I did find someone. **Four people,** in fact. Although I use the term "**people**" loosely.

"You shouldn't be out this late," Pebble said, sneering at me.

"**Yeah,**" Donkey said. "**It's dangerous.**"

Then Rock grabbed me by one shoulder. Sap grabbed me by the other. I tried to break free, of course, but they were **too strong.** It didn't matter. We'd done all of this before. I do something to make Pebble angry, and he and his friends dunk me in a well. It's like a routine now. **What timing, though, huh?** I didn't even have to wait a day to try out **my new hood!**

Maybe that was why I didn't struggle so much. I couldn't wait to see the look on Pebble's face.

I imagined it all in my head. After they **threw me** down the well, I'd swim to the bottom. Minutes later, I'd swim back up and tell them how nice it is down there, **how comfortable, how relaxing,** then swim back down again. **A perfect plan.** A perfect way to make Pebble **even angrier.** And that would have been great . . . if they'd **taken me to a well.**

However . . .
THAT'S <u>DEFINITELY</u> NOT A WELL.

They took me to an area by **the east wall.** No one lives there.
After sunset, it's **a lonely place,** besides the guards standing watch.

No, this place isn't **scary at all.** It's for a surprise party, **right?**

We stopped in front of **a storage room.** Specifically, a **dirt** and **cobblestone** storage room. A lonely little shack that only the miners visit. A building of **low importance,** built against the east wall. I didn't know why they'd brought me here, and I didn't want to find out. I **struggled** again and again, but I might as well have been a rabbit on a **very short leash.**

"We should've taken a lesson from that zombie and made **some weakness potions,**" Donkey said.

Pebble opened the door. The others **shoved** me inside.

"What are you going to do this time?" I asked.

"Make me eat dirt?"

"I guess you could say that. You'll be **flying** first, though."

When they pushed me to the back of the storage room, I . . . suddenly **understood what he meant.**

It's nothing but a normal stockpile. **Yeah . . . that's it!**

16

Pebble must have **removed** the back of the building. Since the storage room was **connected** to the east wall, they could dig a hole into the wall without anyone noticing. Both of Pebble's parents are **miners.** So today, they probably did something to stop any miner from dumping extra materials here.

"**What are you . . . I don't . . .**" I had to struggle for even these words.

When Pebble turned to me, **his eyes were as black as obsidian.** "**You're a danger** to our village, Runt. You'll be **the end** of us all. My father can see it. I can see it. **This has to end now.**"

"Yeah, so you're gonna help everyone out by **blowing up the wall,** huh?!"

"You really **aren't so bright,** are you? Tonight, I'm dropping **two bats with one arrow.** First, I'll no longer have to worry about you. Second . . ."

I already knew what he was going to say. **It was obvious.** He wanted to reclaim his title as the **hero of this village.** Saturday's celebration took him out of the torchlight, which was now shining directly on me. After that TNT went off, not only would I, **his biggest threat,** be removed from the picture, but . . . monsters could then rush in. Which he'd then take care of. A wimpy villager named Runt would become nothing more than **a distant memory.** A villager punk named

Pebble would clean up and become a hero once more. **A savior.**
A leader. A very solid plan.

"**You're totally crazy!**" I snapped, still struggling.

"**Crazy?** After those mobs come pouring in, I'm going to be the best! I'm going to fight them all!! **Every last one!** You'll see!!"

"Actually, he won't," Rock added.

Pebble laughed. "**That's right. Too bad.** You won't get to see any of the changes we're going to make around here."

"Oh, it's so tragic," Sap said. "Poor Runt charged in and **got blown to the Nether and back.** Mayor, sir, we tried to save him, but . . ."

More laughter. Rock stepped into the TNT chamber. "You guys dug the hole **deep enough,** right?"

Hole?
What hole?!

Oh.
That hole.

"Get his pickaxe," Rock said. "**Actually, grab all his tools.** He's a **slippery** little noob."

Then Donkey and Sap took my pickaxe, shovel, and both axes, and were about to take more items until Pebble shouted, "**Hurry up!** We still have to **seal up the wall!** And someone check **the redstone line** again!"

Nice. At least I still had cookies.
Then they threw me <u>into the hole.</u>

"**Farewell, nooblord**," Pebble called out from above me. "I'll make sure to take care of Breeze while you're gone."

As if it couldn't get any worse, Rock placed a **block of explosives** on top of the hole.

19

I was sealed **inside,** three blocks beneath the surface. It reminded me of the emergency shelters they had us dig at school in case we ever got lost outside and couldn't come back before sunset. Except **the blocks surrounding me** were cobblestone, not dirt.

I've been in tight spots before, but this . . .

I could have punched the cobblestone with **my bare hands.** It takes a long time to break a single block that way, though. I heard Pebble's crew sealing up the wall outside, so I guessed I didn't have that long. As always, **I had to think.** Was there a way out of this? **How?**

Well, even if I could **break the TNT** block above me and somehow manage to climb out, I'd still be trapped **within the wall itself.**

Another layer of cobblestone would need to be broken, then, and I no longer had the proper tools. What, was I going to use **a cookie** or something?!

Arrows, pumpkin pie, emeralds, a compass, a water bucket, a bow, some flint and steel. Yeah, that last one was certainly going to help. **It was hopeless.** They were going to **blow me up.** There was nothing I could do about it. I might as well empty my water bucket and **end it** now . . .

Wait.
A water bucket?!

What was it again that old **Professor Snark** said?

Once, we had **a whole class** just on water buckets. He said they were **the best item a warrior could ever have on hand.** Better than an enchanted **obsidian** sword. Better than **Nether dragon-scale armor.** Filled with water, a bucket can save you in a ton of different tricky situations. With it, you could **turn lava into obsidian** . . .

. . . **prevent** falling damage . . .

. . . **hide** from endermen . . .

. . . easily **harvest** seeds . . .

. . . and absorb the damage from **an explosion!**

I emptied that bucket in the space above my head. Water came **rushing** down. The only problem was that I could run out of air, but **my new enchantment** solved that. Actually, I didn't even need it. In less than a minute, explosions tore through the wall.

I still took some damage, in fact.
To tell the truth . . .
I totally blacked out.

Water. When I came to, the first thing I felt was water. I was lying on my back in a shallow, narrow stream—part of the spring I'd created. As I sat up, I was **awestruck. The damage Team Pebble had caused was unbelievable.**

On the wall above me, a human leaned over **a broken edge.**

"Hey! Villager! **You okay down there?**" It was Sami, the boy I'd mentioned before.

"**It was Pebble!**" I shouted. "Did you see where he went?"

"Who?"

Sigh. Never mind. I didn't feel like talking, anyway—too dazed from the health bar drop. I climbed up out of the "**crater.**" Only then did I fully grasp the **extent of the damage.** Besides wrecking the wall, the explosions ended up knocking down many of the torches—which created perfect places for monsters to spawn. **Things were not looking good.**

I swam up the spring and refilled my bucket. The spring shrank down to nothing, just soggy ground. Best item indeed. Moments later, **the note-block alarm system** went off. It was located in a short tower near the center of the village. Even though it was some ways away, the noise was easily heard from here. So **the crafters finally got it figured out,** then. They'd been working on it for weeks. Had even modded the note blocks to make **a special noise.** Some of the

humans say it sounds like a **siren**. **Thunder** followed this alarm, followed by **rain**. A flash of lightning illuminated the area beyond the storeroom.

In that split second, through the gloom, a silhouette could be seen: Pebble's **shadowy form . . .**

He stepped into the torchlight, **sword drawn, cloak blowing in the wind,** rain running down his face.

"I had a feeling you'd survive," he said. "Forgot to remove that **stupid cloak** of yours. **That thing is way too good.**"

My cloak? I'd totally forgotten about it.

Still, there was no way it would have helped me survive something like that.

"You mean OP," I said and **drew my sword.** "Just like me."

That did it. He threw himself at me. I met his blade with mine.

A clash of enchanted iron. We traded blocks for a long time, lightning flickering, thunder booming, alarms blaring, heavy rain pouring down. Our health bars shrank slightly every time we did. But mine was **shrinking faster.** There was no way I could beat him one-on-one. He was **too strong, too fast.** On equal footing, I would lose.

Here I was, fighting one of the best students in school—**one filled with insanity and jealous rage**—yet I'd talked about being more careful only hours ago. **I didn't care. I was angry.** He risked our entire village for his own gain. **I had to fight.** Had to do something besides run away. Had to—

Ouch. My vision flashed bright red. At the same time, there was another flash of iron. My health bar shrank from right to left until only **two hearts** remained. A critical hit. He'd also backed me into a corner. So much for knowing when to run.

His sword came down again, **removing the last of my health bar.** At this point, I didn't even feel pain. **Well played, Pebble. Well played.**

His sword came down **a second time.** This time, it removed the last of my health bar.

"What?!" His sword came down **a third time.**

Okay, this time, it removed the last of my health bar. **Wait, no. Hold on.** He swung again.

Okay, okay—the last of my health bar was definitely taken away this time. **Definitely. No, wait. Sorry. It just went back up.**

"Are you **kidding me?!**" Again and again he swung, and each time **my health bar refilled slightly.** Between each swing, I gained about **three hearts,** more or less **negating the damage he'd inflicted.**

Which meant . . . I was **regenerating?!**

The only thing I know of that gives such a powerful regenerative effect is an **enchanted golden apple.** The cloaks the mayor had rewarded us with apparently had this effect. Or something similar. **It was unbelievable.** Suddenly filled with confidence, I returned Pebble's aggression. Armed with this buff, I simply **couldn't lose.** **The end result was Pebble cowering with half a heart remaining.**

"How did you **use it twice?!** I don't see a full moon!! **That's so unfair!!**"

Like the mobs play fair, I wanted to say, but took out my water bucket and waved it before him.

"So it was like that, huh . . ." He turned away.

I threw the bucket onto the ground in front of him.

"Should've **paid attention** in Mob Defense, **noob.**"

"Yeah, yeah, okay. Go on. **Finish me off. I deserve it.** Besides, I can't face my father after this . . ."

"If I couldn't **do it to a slime,** how could I do it to you? Not that you're any better. You'll be way **more useful** alive, anyway. I'm sure they'll assign you **a lot of fun tasks** . . . after they throw you **in jail.**"

Pebble wasn't listening anymore. He was staring at **the massive** hole he'd created, or perhaps staring through it, **at the** forest beyond.

"What have I done?" he said, his voice wavering. "**What have I done . . . ?**"

The sounds of approaching humans grew louder. They were **riding horses** and arrived before anyone else. Of course, Pebble and I received **strange looks.** Kolbert rode up to us. "Someone said that they saw you two **sneaking** into that building just minutes before the explosion! Care to **explain?**"

Pebble shot up. "**I'm sorry, sir!** I tried to stop him, but he **hurt me** so bad!"

All eyes were on me.

That Pebble. And here I just said that he was on the same level as a slime. After this, I'm moving him all the way down—to that of **creeper potato.** By the way, that's not a vegetable. I guess creepers go to the bathroom, too . . .

"**Please**," Pebble said, "you've got to help me! **He's lost his mind!**"

"What are you talking about?!" Kolbert looked so confused. "Hey! **Runt! What happened here?!**"

28

I ignored him as well. Beyond the blown-up wall, a chorus of moans could be heard, and they were getting **louder by the second.**

There was no time
to explain.

SATURDAY NIGHT—
UPDATE III

The rain was straight out of **an enderman's nightmare.** I could barely hear anything through the heavy downpour. Still, when **I listened closely,** I could hear the eerie cries, long and sad. **The shuffling. The scraping.** The endless, **ragged breathing.**

They were coming.

You see, while attracted to torchlight (and, of course, explosions), zombies are particularly fond of **large holes in cobblestone walls.** Only when the lightning flashed did I understand just **how many there were.**

So many, in fact, that describing their count with a single word, number, phrase, or even sentence, just doesn't feel appropriate. For example, I could say there were a lot of them. But then, to a noob or even a level 50 student, "**a lot**" could mean **three. Instead, I'll provide a little story** to help illustrate what we faced tonight.

Once, in school, we made a **cow farm.** At first, there were only two cows, but their numbers grew and grew. Within a week, **so many cows** were crammed into their little fenced-in area that:

1.) Most cows were **stuck together.**

2.) Many cows were **sticking halfway out** of the fence.

3.) Some cows looked like they had become a **part of the fence.**

4.) Their collective mooing was **so loud** that no one even wanted to go near that farm anymore.

5.) A few cows actually began warping **back and forth,** back and forth, to a spot outside of the fence, **which is just crazy** if you've ever seen that.

Now **imagine a much bigger cow farm**—roughly one-fifth the size of a biome.

Now turn all of those cows into zombies.
Now take away the fence.

That's how many attacked us tonight. What's **stranger** is that they all wore **identical light blue shirts.** Where did they get all that **dye?** Well, some wore mismatched armor, like all gold over a pair of those hideous-looking chain boots. **No class, man. No class.** With gear like that, it was hard **to take them seriously.** *What kind of army is Herobrine sending at us?* I thought. *A bunch of swordless zombies rolling around in chain boots? Really? It's, like, an insult, man!*

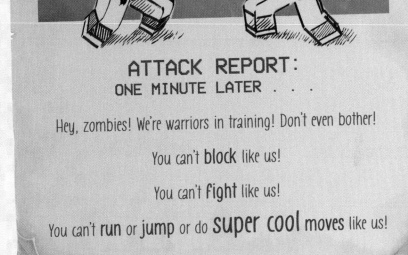

ATTACK REPORT:
ONE MINUTE LATER . . .

Hey, zombies! We're warriors in training! Don't even bother!

You can't **block** like us!

You can't **fight** like us!

You can't **run** or **jump** or do **super cool** moves like us!

This made the zombies **very, very angry,** because they totally wanted to sprint and jump and do cool **special attack moves.** They totally did. Luckily, nearly every kid in school had shown up by then. They arrived **so quietly.** There were few words, **no shouts or commands,** and not the slightest trace of fear. They wanted to be here.

Graduation was coming, their ranks weren't high, and what better way **to improve your combat grade** than battling an endless wave of undead?

To the humans, zombies meant items, **experience points,** and perhaps a way to vent the **frustrations** that came with being trapped in a world of one-meter cubes.

Kolbert pointed his sword at the broken section of wall. '**We'll hold them off there!**'

Oh yes, **we would hold them off there.** We would hold that area like a noob clutching **his first diamond.** If we didn't, a countless number of zombies would spill into the streets, and **game over,** thanks for playing. They'd trash everything . . . **including the ice cream stand.**

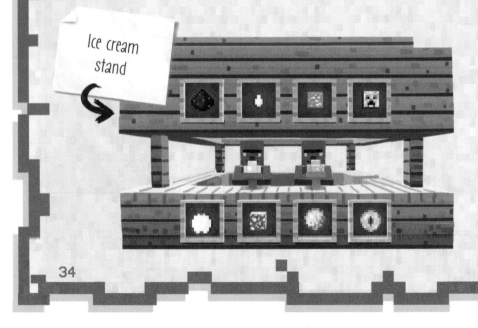

Ice cream
stand

The ice cream stand?!

No! Not the ice cream stand, with its little item frames featuring all eight flavors! **Not that! Anything but that!** Ransack my bedroom, fine! Blow up our fountain, okay! Just don't touch that cute little hut made out of fence and blocks of wood! With it gone, I'd no longer be able to enjoy **diamond ore chunk,** with its perfect texture, its fantastic consistency, and a blend of flavors so utterly amazing it should count as enchanted food! How could they destroy that?! How could they?!

They might be monsters, but **even they have limits, right?** Even they should know where to draw the line!

I bit into a cookie without taking **my eyes off the enemy. No way** were they getting past us tonight.

All we had to do was block this entry point, and their numbers **wouldn't matter.** We also had to pray to Notch that they weren't backed by **endercreepers.** Oh. And we also had to swing.

Experience points swirled through the air in colorful streams. The smoke from **so many dissolving bodies** made it difficult to see.

Arrows, sent from the rooftops, practically outnumbered the raindrops.

Mean
=
red

Nice
=
green

Brio was somehow wielding **two swords at once.** Drill was using **an iron axe enchanted with Smite V.** Breeze only landed critical hits, her feet rarely touching the ground. Emerald and Kolbert were fighting side by side as if they were best friends. And Max and Stump were about to fight the **creepiest zombie ever—it had black skin and glowing green eyes.**

Stump's eyes were almost as **wide** as cookies. "**W-what is that?!**"

"A ghoul, I think." Max adjusted his glasses. "That's what happens when a zombie . . . never mind. Just don't let it touch you."

"In the name of Notch, you can count on that!"

The mayor had even drawn his gold sword, which was unenchanted—more of a ceremonial piece than an actual weapon. That's when you know things are bad. Of course, in the very front fought Pebble. Of course! And what a hero he was! There were times when he jumped in front of villagers or humans to save them. There were times when he took out a zombie with a single, critical hit. There were times when he nudged someone aside to take out even more.

And all of this was done in a flashy way, to draw more attention to himself.

So brave!
So fearless!
Look at him go!

Every so often, he glared at me. I was just glad he kept his distance. Truth be told, part of me secretly wanted to shove him into the zombies. How could he blow up the wall? How could he try to blow me up? I always knew he was a jerk, but dude . . . is he Herobrine's kid or something?!

More important, what was going to happen **after the battle?** Would everyone believe him? **Most likely.** After all, he had his friends to back him up. **But that didn't matter now.** If the mobs forced us back into the streets . . .

You can have any flavor you like . . . as long as it's slime.

My anger only grew. One after **another,** the zombies fell like anvils. Every time I dropped one, though, another stepped in to fill its place.

It went on like this for a long time. My arms got **tired.** It almost felt like I was debuffed with **mining fatigue.**

ATTACK REPORT:
THIRTY MINUTES LATER . . .

"You . . . holding . . . on?"
"Yeah . . . "

Yeah, Stump and I **were totally exhausted.** My mind wandered at times. I'm not proud of this, but once, I . . . I started wondering if it's possible **to build a house out of cake.**

SATURDAY NIGHT— UPDATE IV

Ninety-four zombies,
ninety-five, ninety-six, ninety-seven . . .
Cake . . . castle . . . ?
Err—ninety-eight, ninety-nine . . .

I was about to hit **one hundred** when another student bumped into me. He dashed forward one block and **finished off the zombie** I'd been working on.

I glared at him. **'Hurrr! You kill stealer!'**

"**Kill stealer?!**" He laughed. "This is my spot, cobblehead! **Go somewhere else!**"

Of course, I knew this kid. **Cogboggle.**

Another annoying punk, just like Pebble.

Styled brows and multicolored robes: the latest in villager punk fashion.

For the longest time, his rank wasn't all that high. Somewhere in the middle, **66th or 67th.**

But after he heard about the **Path of the Diamond,** he did anything he could to get ahead. That was why he stole my kill. He was just trying to increase his rank, to break into the top. Some say he only wants to become **a captain** so he can boss others around. **I totally believe it.** He's ruthless, both a scammer and a thief. He cares only about emeralds, items, and ripping off others.

If he was a captain, he could force the students under him to give him all kinds of "**gifts**" and "**donations.**"

With that in mind, I should have been careful around him, but I wasn't going to let him get away with this. He took my zombie, that punk! So I shoved him aside . . . and stole one of his.

"**You little noob,**" he hissed, and shoved me back.

Soon, we were all but wrestling, nudging and shoving and kicking and pushing each other while fighting the zombies before us. Once, I even **stomped on his foot.**

"Dirtface!"

"Noobking!"

"Blockhead!"

"Worthless crafter!"

"Slime nugget!"

"Enderbutt!"

41

"Bat farmer!"

Bat farmer?! **Now that was just going too far!** I stepped back and let him have his zombie. Then, just as he was about to deal the final blow, **I whipped out my bow and stole his kill.**

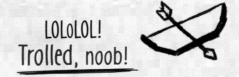

**LOLoLOL!
Trolled, noob!**

He actually thought he was going to get that zombie! He thought that! **He did!** The look on his face . . . **WOW.** I tried to draw it but I couldn't stop laughing.

He was super angry. "You know, after my crew passes yours in rank, I'll make sure Breeze gets **placed under my command!** I'll make her do all the dirty work! **I'll put her on a leash!**"

With one last **"Hurrr!"** he stormed off, no doubt to go steal some other kid's mobs.

Why did he have to bring Breeze into this?! I started to **go after him.** Then I felt a hand on my shoulder—**as soft as Silk Touch.**

"Forget about him," Breeze said. "Focus. **We're losing.**"

SATURDAY NIGHT—
UPDATE V

At first, I didn't get what she was saying.

Stump didn't, either. "Who's losing?!" he shouted, a few blocks away.

"The only thing I'm losing is inventory space," Emerald said. "Just wish they'd drop something useful."

Then the realization came, slowly at first, and then faster and faster, like a mine cart gathering speed, until *boom.*

I glanced down at my sword. **It only had around 50% durability.** In addition, the zombies actually managed to hit us from time to time. Due to **our fatigue,** we'd all grown careless. My own life bar was at eight hearts. This meant our weapons—and our very lives— were slowly wearing down. Throw enough zombies at us, one lifeless body after another, and we'd eventually break.

Everyone else around me seemed to realize this as well. There wasn't much talking before, but now . . . **no one said a word.**

Breeze fought even harder and cut through zombies with **impressive speed**—and **just as quickly,** more shambled up to replace them. Pebble somehow matched her. His speed was insane tonight! Yet in his bravado, he took several hits from the side, and drank a **Healing I** like he was in a potion-chugging contest. Then the mayor's **sword broke**

over a zombie's head. He glanced down at the golden cubes scattered across the ground, as if his sword had been our only hope.

"Oh dear."

Oh dear?

He brought a gold sword

into battle and all he could say was, "**Oh dear**"?

Yeah. **It was over.** It seemed that Villagetown would soon come to an end. Our amazing village, the last line of defense for thousands of blocks around, was going to fall.

The **most ridiculous thing** was that the monsters had nothing to do with it. It was all thanks to **one of our top students.**

Then, just when I thought it couldn't get any worse, **Kolbert left the front line.** Without saying a single word, he just turned around and casually walked away. Emerald gave the human a backward glance. You could almost hear her heart shattering like a pink stained-glass block.

"**Wow,**" she said. "I can't believe he just . . . **wait, what's he doing?**"

More of us glanced back at him. The scarf-wearing knight had an **annoyed look** on his face. "**Are you guys noobs or what . . . ?**" he muttered.

Then he did **something legendary.**

Something that no villager will ever forget.

Something epic, amazing, unimaginably cool, and at first, a little bit confusing.

Kolbert put away his sword and . . .
from his inventory, retrieved . . .
an <u>enchanted</u> golden shovel.

I know, I know. That doesn't sound **so legendary.** We were just as confused. We gave him the **strangest looks.** A few kids I barely knew even made rude comments:

"A golden shovel?!"

"Um, 'lol'?"

"And he's the one asking if we're noobs?"

"Hurrr. Poor guy finally cracked. **He's totally lost it!"**

If it had been anyone else, I'm sure Emerald would have made some comment, but now **she was totally silent.** The sight of Kolbert standing there, golden shovel in hand, rendered me speechless as well. **It was too ridiculous. Too noob.**

Kolbert—the guy who's always talking about how his sword will one day become very close friends with Herobrine—had stopped fighting to . . . **dig?**

I just couldn't **understand.** The thing that baffled me the most was the shovel. A golden shovel. It was enchanted, yeah, okay, okay, sure, but it was still made of gold.

Gold! Not iron or diamond or **elementium** or some other **rare material** we've only read about. Honestly, when it comes to tools, even wood is superior.

In school, we learned that gold has roughly **half the durability** of wood. So it just didn't make any sense. Honestly, maybe the only thing a golden shovel has going for it is . . . **um. Digging speed?**

Okay, sure. A golden shovel equals or surpasses a diamond one in every known material.

On top of that, I'm guessing his shovel was enchanted with **Efficiency III,** the way it was glowing.

Cool, **so he could dig super fast**—but what was he going to do with all that speed? **Make an underground village?**

As I glanced back at him, wondering what was coming next, Kolbert **tore through the dirt** beneath his enchanted iron boots. And I mean **tore.**

Like **diamond through sand.** Like an enderdragon through . . . anything. Like me with **presents,** which is arguably the fastest known speed in all four dimensions.

A human named **Trevor3419** quickly noticed the dirt flying everywhere. "**Hey guys!**" he called out. "Look! Kolbert's trying out his new strat!"

Huh? New strat?
What's he talking about?
What's he going to do?

I was so **curious,** it was hard paying attention to the zombies in front of me. Hey, zombies, can you guys just stop attacking for a second? **I really want to see what's going on back there!**

Of course, I've been around humans long enough to know that Trevor3419 was referring to a strategy of some kind, but I still didn't fully understand. More humans left the front line, then. **Trevor3419, Alex, Julian, Emmie, AquaCraze, Calla, TreyR9, Ninja Jack, Simone . . .** Wielding their gold shovels, they jumped into the pit Kolbert had created.

As they carved their way through so much grass and dirt, their strategy became clear.

Team Golden Shovel. They dig faster than their own shadows.

They were digging a moat: a wide pit that would prevent the zombies from advancing any farther. Zombies **can't jump,** you see. They can hop up to a higher block, but they can't even **jump across a one-block gap.** There could have been one million zombies out there, but with that moat in place, it wouldn't matter anymore. **It was a brilliant plan**—err, strat.

Strategy 11:
emergency ditch

This is what the moat would
look like, once complete.
(The green area represents the
bottom of the moat.)

However, there was still one problem: Even with enchanted
gold shovels, they needed more **time.** The front line had to hold off the
zombies long enough for **Team Golden Shovel** to finish digging.

49

Drill understood this, and resumed being Drill. **"Protect those humans!!** Hold that line like bedrock!! Swing faster than doors connected to redstone torches!!"

Okay, so he lost me on that last one. I'm guessing doors connected to redstone torches swing pretty fast or something?

Um . . . whatever. **Let's just say we followed our orders.**

"I think even bedrock would crack if a thousand zombies were standing on it."
—Stump

All of us were tired. Most of us were wounded and **out of food.** Some were forced to use axes after their swords broke.

The zombies grew **more relentless,** and more of those **creepy-looking things** with black skin and green eyes were showing up. **Ghouls.** They're **very rare** and **powerful,** like the zombie version of a charged creeper. According to legend, they inflict a status effect—**which is worse than that of any wither skeleton.**

GHOUL

LIFE
???

ARMOR
???

SPEED
???

INTELLIGENCE
???

SPECIAL POWERS:
WEAKENING, BY TOUCH,
EFFECT UNKNOWN

Ghoul data sheet. Notice the complete lack of information. Maybe its status effect hurts you really bad. Maybe it turns you into pumpkin pie. We really need to hit the ancient libraries more often.

51

Also, well, I don't want to write about this, but . . . a few of the zombies **wore robes. Former villagers.** They must have come from distant villages. **I dropped a few myself . . .**

Even though they were no longer like us, I felt **guilty** every time I did. Once, after one of them fell, the only item he left behind was **a fishing rod.** He must 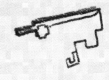 have liked fishing . . . before he became a zombie. I still can't get this memory out of my head. Obviously, some of us in the front line had trouble fighting them after that. It was something that **had to be done,** but at the same time . . .

Whenever I looked into their eyes, I wondered what their village was once like, what their old lives had been like, and how they had come to see living creatures the way I see **pumpkin pie.**

Had they never built walls? **Had they refused to craft weapons?** Had they simply hidden within their houses, praying for an early sunrise?

Their presence even **affected Pebble.** He actually avoided them, and let others take care of them. Every time he encountered one, **he began sweating,** his face became as white as a ghast's, and he shivered, hands trembling, as if a cave spider's debuff were running through his veins.

Maybe it was sinking into that obsidian-thick head of his.

Maybe he realized that, **because of his actions,** the same thing might happen here. Maybe that was why, after about the ninth or tenth green villager arrived, he . . . **suddenly charged in.**

Before anyone could say anything, he was **three blocks ahead of Breeze and me.** My friends rushed in to help him. They weren't exactly rooting for **Team Pebble,** but they didn't know about what had happened earlier, either.

"**What are you doing?!**" Breeze snapped.

Stump cut down a zombie to Pebble's left. "**Are you crazy?! Get back, noob!**"

"W-we can't let them get us!!" he shouted, swinging frantically. "**We won't!! We can't!!**

W-we'll get them all!!"

Zombies swarmed everywhere to our **left and right.** We shouldn't have been this far ahead. **It was too dangerous.** Pebble didn't seem to care. He just waded through them. He cut them down, left and right, left and right, but there were **just so many.**

That was when I noticed the black zombie only one block to Pebble's right. This close, I could see the green particles dripping from its skin, similar to **a slime's ooze,** just like in the ghost stories.

It was reaching for him, **slow and feeble,** and suddenly I recalled some tale about a villager who'd once been touched by one, hundreds of years ago.

It almost got him . . .

I don't know why I saved him. **It didn't involve thinking.** My arms moved automatically. My sword flew as if forced by a piston. **The ghoul flew back.**

I saved him. I saved Pebble without a second thought, without any hesitation, as if I were saving my best friend, despite everything he had done to me . . .

Pebble stared at me over his shoulder,
face twisted in **disbelief.**

·Thanks.·

Long story short, **we won.**

The humans **finished digging.** The front line jumped over. Others poured lava in.

Boom, there you have it—the recipe for **sad zombies.** Kolbert's strat worked **perfectly.**

Of course, if this had happened months ago, the zombies would have pushed each other forward until the ones in front fell into the moat. But they are **much, much smarter now.** They stopped immediately.

Then they just stood there, looking at us pitifully, and sometimes moaned. Not one of them dropped into the lava. *(For a zombie, that's really smart, okay?)* I even expected at least one of them to place a **dirt block** to form a bridge, but nope.

They've improved, but apparently they still have a long way to go before graduating from Mob Academy . . .

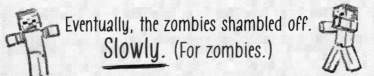 Eventually, the zombies shambled off. <u>Slowly.</u> (For zombies.)

We watched them retreat back into the gloom, into the plains, toward their crummy little forest.

Then the cheers grew louder than a creeper blast. Twenty or so villagers **rushed over to Kolbert** and his friends, praising them, asking tons of questions. Brio even **shook Kolbert's hand.**

Not everyone was so upbeat, though. Many who'd fought in the front line were **too tired to break out their villager dance moves.**

My friends and I regrouped near the **blown-up building** that was once the miner's storeroom.

"We shouldn't cheer just yet," Emerald said. "I mean, moats might work now, but there will probably come a day when zombies can **jump, even fly.**"

Breeze leaned against one of the storeroom's broken walls. "Thankfully, today isn't that day."

"This would have been much easier if we'd just dumped lava **at the entrance points,**" Max said. "I'll make a note of this in my records." *(Yes, Max has a diary now, too.)*

I was one of **the only kids** here who didn't say a word. The other one was **Pebble.** He was staring at the ground, totally still.

Then he approached. Surprisingly, I didn't detect the slightest trace of anger.

"**Runt, uh . . .**" He avoided my gaze as if I were the king of the endermen. "**Can we, um . . . talk?**"

I looked away.

Long ago, I would have **raged hard.** My blood would have been boiling like a potion on a brewing stand. Had I been indoors, I would have shot through a cobblestone roof. But now **I was calm—** as calm as a skeleton in a world without dogs. Which was strange, honestly, because I'd eaten way too many cookies before battle. **Way too many.**

I nodded. "Yeah."

Then Pebble took off. I followed, leaving my friends behind. They were totally speechless. They gave me **the weirdest looks,** like I was trying to craft using my inventory—and not the two-by-two-block grid, mind you, but actual inventory space.

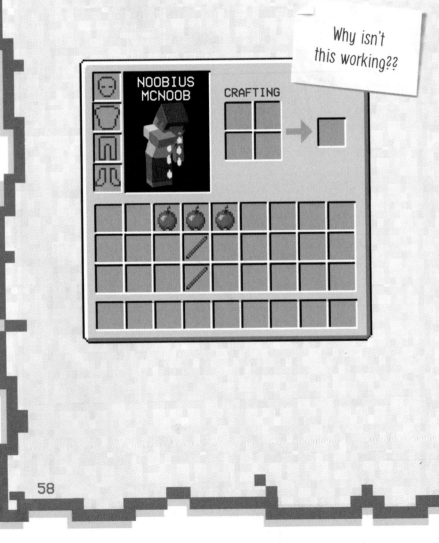

Why isn't this working??

NOOBIUS MCNOOB

CRAFTING

After we gained some distance from the crowd, **Pebble turned to me.**

"I was **wrong** about you," he said. "Totally, **totally wrong.** I know this won't fix anything, and **I know you'll never forgive me, but . . . I'm . . . sorry.** You're a good guy."

"Yeah, and I'm sure you're going to say the **exact same thing to the mayor**," I said.

He gave me a single, slow nod. "I am. Look, I don't know what happened. **I just wasn't myself!** I might've been a **jerk** to you lately, but even you know I'm not like that!"

". . ."

"And I thought you were a spy!" he blurted out. "I saw your pet! **A baby slime!** So I thought you'd turned on us, and when you became a war hero, I just . . . **snapped**."

"Then you should've talked to me about it," I said. "**Or reported me.** Something. **Anything but THIS!** I mean, do you have any idea what's in store for you once the mayor learns the truth?"

"**I know.** Believe me, I know." He reached into his inventory. "That's why . . . you should take this."

He threw a **stack of emeralds** onto the ground, followed by **five more.** He then emptied out the **rest of his inventory,** including

59

enchanted tools. In utter disbelief, I watched as he threw down each of his items, **one by one.** Finally, he added his armor, sword, and cloak to the mix.

"**All yours,**" he said. "Oh. I have more stuff at home. We can go there now, if you want."

What is this? I gazed down at the **gleaming, glittering, glowing pile of items.** He sure had some real loot. **Three diamonds.** A ton of emeralds. **A golden apple.** Several potions. A fishing rod with **Dredge I.** Even Mobspanker, **his enchanted bow.**

WOW, I thought. *Is this a trick or something? Why is he giving me all his stuff? And what's that Dredge enchantment?!*

I shook my head. "What are you doing?!"

He sighed. "**Come on,** it's not like I'm gonna need them anymore. If you don't take them, they'll just wind up in a storeroom somewhere. **You know that.**"

" . . . "

Jail, I thought. *He's talking about jail!* Yeah, that's the **standard punishment** around here. But there is a worse punishment, one **reserved for traitors** like him. Maybe Pebble wasn't aware of that, but I was—I've learned a lot from hanging out with Max.

Still, the last time that happened to anyone was over a hundred years ago. Surely the mayor wouldn't . . .

No, I thought, *the mayor isn't that cruel.* I wouldn't wish that fate on anyone, even someone like Pebble.

Pebble shrugged. "Fine, **let someone else have them.** Time to get this over with. Guess this is **good-bye.**"

I didn't say anything, just gave him **the coldest look.** I had to be careful, I felt. I assumed he was going to try **something crazy.**

He turned his back to me. "I just want you to know, I did what I thought was best for the village, and I'm . . . **about to do the same thing, now.**"

Then he took off in the direction of the mayor. **Head low. Face grim.** But his shoulders were still high. His steps came heavy as he walked through the cheerful crowd.

Maybe I should have **stopped** him.

It's hard to believe, but . . .
Pebble is gone.

The mayor's words are still fresh in my mind: ". . . **destruction** of village property, attempted **murder**, violation of—oh, enough with this mumbo jumbo! **Pebble Graybanner**, you are hereby **banished** from our village **until the Nether freezes over!!**"

The worst part was Pebble had dropped **all of his items.** He was sent out there, totally alone, and **didn't have any items.** Not even a block of wood.

Despite what he had done to me, I almost feel sorry for him. There's no way he'll make it even one day. Five months ago, sure, he would have been fine, but now . . . **he doesn't stand a chance.**

As for Pebble's friends, **they were thrown in jail.** Pebble pleaded, begged, and told the mayor it was all his idea.

I'm not sure how long they'll be locked up. Maybe a month, **maybe longer.**

By the way, Pebble's father was furious about the whole thing. **He disowned Pebble.**

"My son has disgraced our family name," he said. "I'll never forgive him for what he's done!"

Many villagers stood on either side of him. Pebble's entire extended family. Most were miners. You could tell by the dark, earth tones of their robes. Their faces were darker.

At least a few people have suggested that Pebble's father isn't exactly a nice guy. Yet here he was, on the verge of tears. Acting?

Whatever,
I was too tired to care.

This morning, there was a **celebration.** If you could call it that. No one cheered. The mayor didn't say much about the mobs. He did have some **good news,** however.

"This year, the students have exceeded **our wildest expectations,**" he said. "This may come as a shock, but . . . most of you have **advanced past one hundred** in at least one skill."

The mayor went on to tell us that **we're able to go past 100%** in any given skill. It's always been this way. But the record books were capped before. **They only displayed a maximum of 100%.** The teachers never expected us to do this well. Last year, **the highest level any student attained was 82%.** Due to the war, the students have been pushed hard this year.

It's not that surprising, honestly. Long ago, I wrote about how 100% represents competency. Competency means you're capable of doing the job. It's not the same thing as mastery.

Most blacksmiths are skilled crafters, yes. But what about some **legendary** old blacksmith who lives in the mountains and can forge blades with his beard? His skill might be **500%** or more.

"Your books should be updated by now," the mayor said. "Go on, **take a look.**"

I glanced down at my record book
<u>in shock.</u>

RUNT
STUDENT
LEVEL 106

MINING	99%
COMBAT	107%
TRADING	101%
FARMING	99%
BUILDING	102%
CRAFTING	98%

There were a lot of gasps around me. It sounded like a lot of kids had raised at least **one skill beyond 100%.** Breeze is still ahead of me, **of course.** Not that I expected anything less from a former **test subject of Herobrine's.**

BREEZE
STUDENT
LEVEL 109

MINING	101%
COMBAT	117%
TRADING	101%
FARMING	125%
BUILDING	102%
CRAFTING	106%

How and why is her farming score so high?! What's up with that?! I'll have to ask her . . .

Once the mayor was finished, Drill talked about the **Path of the Sword.** He said students who choose this path will be divided equally among the **five captains.** So if **fifty take up the sword,** each captain will be responsible for **ten warriors.**

The best part about this is that friends will be assigned with friends. Meaning, if I become a captain and Stump chooses warrior, **we'll be working together, no matter what.**

A lot of kids cheered at this news.

Then Brio ruined everyone's mood. He said there will be **four more tests** before graduation:

1) **A mining test.** It was postponed for ages, but now it's finally here.
2.) **A combat test** in the form of a single-elimination tournament known as Ice Cup.
3.) **A redstone test.** I don't know anything about redstone. Stump knows a little, but he's out of ideas after that last test.
4.) **The final.** Students must submit ideas on how to get revenge against the mobs. The teachers will select the best idea. The students will carry it out.

Hurgg.

A redstone test?! Why did they have to pull a trick like this? Redstone hasn't been taught that much in school!

"At least **the final will be easy**," Emerald said. "Revenge? Hand me that **flint and steel** and follow me to their forest; I'll show you revenge!"

Breeze **giggled**. "The tournament **sounds fun,** too. How will that work?"

"We'll be playing **Skyball**," Stump said, and then he went over the rules of this villager game.

Skyball **is tough.** You have two teams with six players each, and everyone's **taking snowballs to the face.** Supposedly, there's a huge village far to the west where they take these games way more seriously than we do. They hold an annual tournament there known as **Legendary Cup.** The **best players are like heroes,** respected even more than warriors.

As Stump talked about Skyball's finer points, Max got real close to me. He leaned in right next to my ear and whispered: **"How about you and I take a little walk."**

Max told me something **interesting.** It's something his buddy Razberry came up with. **Operation Snoop,** they're calling it.

Basically, Razberry has been going around school and peeking at other kid's record books.

For the past week, he's spent all of his time snooping around like this. **He's not even studying anymore.**

Why is he doing this? **Because he wants to help us out.** You see, Razberry knows he'll never become a captain. **He's going to be a warrior,** though. So he wants to make sure that at least one member of **Team Runt** is able to choose the **Path of the Diamond.** In return, he'll join us after graduation. A lot of the other potential captains are **jerks.** He doesn't want to get stuck under one of them.

I think it will work because nobody really suspects Razberry of anything. I **feel a little bad** for him, though, since he's sacrificing his grades to do this. But then, when it comes to the **Path of the Sword**, grades no longer matter. Even someone like Bumbi could be a warrior and his combat score is still around 20%.

From now on,
Razberry will give us a little list called a level report,
which is pretty much a <u>list of students' levels</u>
to show us where we stand in ranking.

The "celebration" was finally over. My friends and I trudged off to the ice cream stand. We got our cones and sat around one of the many fence-and-wool tables. Breeze suggested we go here to cheer us up. Didn't work for me. Today, even diamond ore chunk was like **moss-covered cobblestone in my mouth.**

"I still can't believe what Kolbert did!" Stump said. "**What a legend,** cleaning up Pebble's **mess** the way he did! And with a trash-tier item, at that!"

When he mentioned Pebble, I must have appeared **even sadder** than before because Breeze tapped me on the shoulder.

"**Hey, don't let it get to you,**" she said. "Pebble got everything he deserved."

I sighed. "I know, but still . . . I just can't help but **feel bad** for some reason. I don't know."

"**Dude, he tried to blow you up!**" Stump said. "You almost found out what it's like to be a creeper! And here I was, **trying to protect him!!**"

Max closed a book he'd been reading called *Village Law.* "I have a feeling he'll make it somehow. **Jerk or not,** he was a **top-ranking student.**"

"Which reminds me," Emerald said. "We're wasting time. Graduation is soon, guys. We should really be **focusing on our studies.**"

"**She's right.**" Breeze stared down at her ghast tear swirl. "**There's still a lot of competition out there.**"

"Not that you should be worrying," Emerald added.

Breeze shrugged. "Truth is, **I'm as clueless about redstone as the rest of you.** I'm afraid Stump will have to carry us again."

"We can all try to come up with something," Stump said. "We'd better, because **Cogboggle** is really rising in rank! **Block, too!** We can't let those punks get ahead!"

Hurgg again.

Graduation is coming.

That Cogboggle kid is just a few levels **behind me.** Pretty much every student is around level 90 by now. **Pebble's gang** might be out of the picture, but just like with the zombies, more will step in to fill their place. I'm sure of it.

By the way, I'd say Cogboggle's even worse than Pebble. At least Pebble seemed to care about the village. **At least Pebble was smart.**

Block is just as bad. After hearing about the **Path of the Diamond,** the two of them began stealing ideas from other kids to do better on tests.

They're not the only ones, either. Kids are desperate these days. They'll do anything for better grades. A lot of them want to be a captain. I mean, **how cool would that be?**

So if I lose focus, some of them could pass me by just days before graduation.

With Operation Snoop in place, though, at least I'll have a warning.

Our best agents are on the case!
Our best! Guaranteed!

Breeze **finally tried** her ice cream. Some of it got on her nose. She didn't seem to notice, however.

Everyone else tried to **hide their grins.**

"What's so funny?! **Oh.**" Breeze's face **turned pink** like the horizon just before dawn. "**Oops.**"

Stump laughed. "I don't get you, Breeze. **You're the best student,** yet you can't eat ice cream properly?"

"Don't worry," Max said. "Runt and Stump can help you out. **They have lots of knowledge on the subject.**"

I couldn't help but join in on the **laughter.** But soon, my gaze **returned** to the distant wall.

Even though I couldn't see past it from here, I imagined the **wilderness and the vast emptiness** that stretched beyond. Lately, the wall guards have been **spotting monsters out there in the daytime.** Ones that have no business underneath the sun.

Kolbert said that he had looked out there the other day and seen a group of zombies wearing enchanted helmets. Those helmets were most likely enchanted with **Unbreaking.** If all of them were equipped with helmets like that, they wouldn't even need their little forest anymore. They could roam for hours **without a cloud in the sky.** And then Sami said he saw **a spider chasing a rabbit** faster than a pig chasing a carrot on a stick. In the daytime. If what he said is true, the spider wasn't **blinded** by the sun.

Um . . .
Farewell, Pebble.
Hope you're having fun.

My friends took off. They all had something to do.

Stump had to help his parents. Max wanted to hit the **library.** Emerald was going to **dinner with her father and a few humans.** *(Including Kolbert, I'm sure.)*

At last, it was just Breeze and me.

"**I want you to take these,**" she said. "You should carry at least a few. **Never know when you might need them.**"

She can be so sweet sometimes, huh? She must have gotten that from her mother, because she's nothing like Brio.

"**Thanks a lot,**" I said. "This human named **Yoonsung** sometimes gets on me to craft or trade for some. **I keep forgetting**, though."

She smiled. "Speaking of humans, I've been wondering . . . why do **so many** of the humans have **numbers after their names?**"

Hurmm.
Good question.

Kolbert's name is really **Kolbert21337**, for example. Then there's **CrafterBot6000, Blaze7381, Meza8, TreyR9,** and **AngryPineapple123,** although they just call him **Pineapple.**

Why do they have numbers in their names? **It's so strange.** If I change my name to **OverlordRunt77777,** will the humans think I'm cool?

"Maybe those numbers are like their **levels** or something," I said with a shrug.

"Wait! So Kolbert is **level 21,337?!**" I added.

"Maybe that's why he's their leader?" She shrugged as well. "Oh, hey, I've been wanting to ask you . . . **have you had any more dreams lately?**"

"Not really. You?"

"Yes. That **wither skeleton** keeps bugging me."

"I'm guessing he asked you to save him," I said.

She nodded. "**Must be the fifth time I've dreamed about him.**"

So strange. Can endermen really control dreams? That wither skeleton must be friends with one.

He's stranded on a block of Netherrack in an ocean of lava. **Whatever.** Not like we can take a trip to the Nether or anything. **Or can we?**

I thought about this for a moment, a **mischievous** grin beginning to form on my face . . .

Breeze's voice tore me from my thoughts. "**Another thing.** I'm . . . the top student, **right?** If that doesn't change, I could **become a captain,** and if I did . . ."

I knew where she was going with this. According to what we heard, a captain will have **a group of students** under his or her command. Maybe they'll be wall guards, maybe scouts, who knows, but they'll work together.

So if **I become a captain,** and Breeze becomes a captain . . . we'll no longer see each other as much. **Worse,** we'll be working with kids we don't know very well. We'll be trusting those kids **with our lives.**

"**We need to make another promise,**" Breeze said. "Otherwise, we might break our first."

I remembered the promise we'd both made.

No matter what, we will always protect each other.

"I don't care if they send me out there," I said, "but . . . not without you, Breeze. **I couldn't do it.**"

And so, we put our hands together. **We made a pact.**

"Even if we both make the cut," she said, "only one of us will choose the **Path of the Diamond. Agreed?**"

"**Agreed.** I don't know if the mayor will get angry at our decision . . . **but it's our decision to make.** Nothing will separate us."

"Nothing."

We went for a walk in the park. Every time I visit that place, I forget about all the stuff going on.

When you're there, **bad memories fade away** as if it were all **really just a bad dream.**

Brilliant sunlight streaming down. Vibrant flowers all around. It's **hard to believe** monsters share a world with a paradise such as this.

For the record, **Breeze and I didn't hold hands! We put our hands together,** which is just something you do when making a big promise like that!

Later, she left to speak with her father about something. She wouldn't tell me what, and I didn't pry. It seemed like she—

Huh?
For some reason,
my quill stopped writing.
Let me try again.

Okay, so, Breeze seemed—

Um, wow. My quill is defective or something. **Hurmm.** I see. Its durability is **almost out.** I've been writing way too much lately. Of course, I could **repair it myself,** but why waste the experience points? I can just **trade a potato for a new one.** I have to save every last point so I can enchant a diamond sword. I almost regret not taking **Pebble's diamonds,** that's how bad I want one.

Sometimes, I can't stop thinking about it. **Have you ever seen a diamond sword in real life?** The edge is so **perfect**, the point so **sharp**, all sea blue shades with **a light violet sheen.**

Trust me, you'll find nothing more beautiful in the Overworld. **Well, besides Breeze.**

. . . ?!
Did I just write that?!

No, real warriors don't get all **mushy like that.** Surely it's this quill.

Yeah, that's it. This quill is acting up. It made me write the wrong thing because **it only has a single point of durab—**

I'm back. I went to a library and traded for a **new** quill.

"Notice that the quills in this world are different from the video game. They aren't very durable in the game. It's almost as if . . . this world were real. Actually, it's Entity303's fault. We would have never had to go to this video game convention. How did he make all this?"

"After I slipped into that virtual reality gear . . . I found myself here."

—Kolbert

Sorry, Kolbert added that.

He said there's **too much mystery** behind the humans arriving in this world. They were at some kind of **special event,** I guess, with some **new kind of Earth machines.** At one point they **blacked out,** and . . . woke up here.

Kolbert told me the whole story, **but I didn't understand most of it.** Although he thinks this is real, he also thinks it has something to do with their machines . . . ?

Entity 303 is supposed to be **some guy who helped make the game, or something . . . ?**

Anyway.

I traded for a new quill. And some cookies. And some cake. And some pumpkin pie, **because why not?** All of that trading got me thinking. There's a **redstone test** coming up. Why not pick up some dust? The best place to get redstone is in this massive building that's just two streets from the library. It's called **"the garage."** It has huge, **piston-operated doors** that are big enough for even an iron golem to enter.

What a mess . . .
I guess Steve and
Mike forgot to clean
up before leaving.

It's basically a **testing area.** Ground zero for redstone **experiments.** Up until they left, Steve and Mike had been working here. Now that they're gone, it's mostly empty. Sometimes, a few humans come in and work on stuff. Not **too many** villagers come here, though. Only a handful.

Redstone is a new field for us.
Uncharted territory.

To most of the older villagers, **like my parents,** a circuit is more **mysterious** than a sword.

"Listen up. You connect the trail of powder to . . . things that will . . . make things."
"You'll also need another thing to . . . power the things."

That's why we don't have redstone grades, and why we rarely attend redstone class. It's so unknown to us that we don't even have real teachers for it. I glanced at the various items **scattered around. They were so strange.** I didn't know how to craft any of them, let alone use them. Redstone dust is used to make circuits, I thought, but you also need . . . other . . . things, right? **Hurgg!!** I'm such a noob with this stuff! **I sound just like Mr. Glowstone!**

Well, Drill had said something about redstone torches. Actually, I didn't know such an item existed until he mentioned them.

How humiliating. He's older than my parents, but he knows way more about this stuff than I do. Comparators . . . repeaters . . . signal locking . . .

I wouldn't know where to begin! **Man, what am I going to do?**

We made a redstone alarm system earlier, but Stump was behind that. He had to help me explain it when I was writing about it in here. **And that system wasn't very complicated,** by the way. Not nearly as complex as some of the things I've seen the humans make. Stump might be ahead of me in this regard, but compared to the humans **he's a super novice.**

Eyes glazing over, I stood before **a repeater** like a zombie in front of an improperly placed door.

Why are these pistons covered in slime? Are they testing a new monster crusher, or what? This block with the face is creeping me out . . .

I have **two or three days** to turn into a master of redstone science, I thought. **Yeah. That just isn't happening . . . Man!** . . . I never thought redstone would matter at all . . . **and now look at me . . .**

I'm sweating ghast tears just thinking about that test!

I was ready to give up and go back home when, behind me, **there was a loud clang, clang, clang.**

That's a common sound in my village. **An iron golem** was walking nearby. Then I heard a silvery voice, soft and feminine.

"Strange seeing you here!"

Huh?! I whirled around. The iron golem was standing two blocks away. It wasn't the one speaking, though. **A girl was there, too** . . . riding on the golem's left shoulder. **Pretty cool,** I have to say. Although it didn't look very comfortable up there. She **hopped down** from her giant iron pet and smiled. **Such a** strange, **strange girl.**

Nessa. Not the shy girl I used to know. Even her hair color is different!

No one **really talks to her** at school. *(Probably because she skips class a lot.)* She spends most of her time **working with redstone,** I guess. From what I've heard, she'd been working on projects with Steve. Beyond that, **she trains her pet iron golem,** experiments with fireworks, **weird stuff like that.** So throughout school this year, her scores haven't been all that high. She's second to last in rank, **just ahead of Bumbi.** The teachers don't assess our skills with redstone, and Nessa doesn't study the other subjects all that much. The only subject she has a decent score in is **crafting,** as she prefers to craft redstone items herself.

I thought about all this in the blink of an enderman. **Nessa's smile only grew.**

"Although I'm not surprised to see you here," she said, "with the upcoming test! **Need some help,** I take it?"

I sighed. "**Yeah.** Connect a lever to my head with redstone dust and turn my brain off, because thinking about this stuff is actually **starting to hurt.**"

She giggled. "**Don't worry!** I was like that when I first started out! Actually, I'm really glad you stopped by! **I've been meaning to ask you something!**"

"Huh? **What's that?**"

"Well, do you have anything **planned for the test?**"

"I was thinking about something involving redstone du—Uhh, **no. Not really.**"

"I see. How about we make a deal, then, hurmm? I can help you out, and you can . . . help me."

There was something about the way she said that last bit—*help me*—that made me pause. Made me cautious, even. *What could I possibly* help her *with?* I thought. Even if I teach her the basics of combat, going up a few ranks won't matter when you're in second-to-last place . . .

Whatever. I could really use her help. I'm not failing that test. Not for anything. Not when I'm this close . . .

What's the worst thing she could ask for, anyway? Does she want me to be a test subject in some kind of experiment? Maybe to see if a villager can carry a current like redstone dust?

At this point, I'd probably agree. Hook me up and throw that lever! I'm ready!

"Just say it," I said.

"Great!" She flashed a smile brighter than a sea lantern. "First, how about we go get something to eat? Talking requires energy, you see, and my hunger bar is getting pretty low!"

It was **the first time** I'd ever had ice cream **twice in one day.** No, technically it's **six times.** As we sat at the table, Nessa **kept buying me more.** Who could say no to such skillfully crafted cones, with each scoop a mini arctic biome of milk and sugar instead of snow?

Attention:
overheated
energy bar!

(In this world, it's possible to consume too much food, which results in a slow debuff: 10% per point over 10. If the humans ever learn how to craft pizza, zombies will be running circles around them.)

So . . . delicious.

Must . . . k–k–keep . . . eating.

Wait a second.

She's being awfully

nice to me . . .

She asked **a ton** of questions, too. *What was Herobrine like?*
Were you scared? How many zombies did you drop yesterday?
Why do you keep writing in that book?

And finally—

"Well, **about what I wanted to ask** . . . it's about my flying
machine. **Have you heard about that?**"

"You bet."

I showed her my diary and the little drawing mentioning **the shy
girl and the flying machine.**

"**Ha!** Well, I suppose I was a little shy back then! Back at the start of
school, I didn't know anyone!"

Yeah, **she had really changed,** I thought. **Weird.** She was a bit
timid before. Now she's **more bubbly** than a pool full of high-diving
magma cubes.

"Okay," she said, "so I've thought about using my flying machine
design for the **upcoming test.**"

Another smile, **radiant**—her eyes became chevrons.

^^

"I've also considered **letting you use it!**" she said. "You and your friends. Then you guys would surely **win first place,** right?"

Hurgg?! Dirt potion?!
Bane of Air III?! Cookie block?! Melon golem?!
<u>Enchanted creeper potato?!</u>

I was so **shocked,** so stunned, that these incomprehensible thoughts flashed through my mind. Had I still been eating right then, the ice cream equivalent of a **firework rocket** would have flown from my mouth.

She's saying that . . . **she's suggesting** . . . she just said that she wants to . . . she'll let us use her flying machine in the redstone test?!

Wait. Waitwaitwait. Wuh-aaaaittttttttt.
That's quite a big favor, no? So that's why she **invited me for ice cream!** Of course! She was totally trying to **butter me up!** She's probably going to ask me to do something **crazy in return!**

What could it be?! What does she want?! **Does it matter?!**
Anything, anything!! Ask me how to fight a real zombie, just ask. I'll
show you how to turn those things into piles of **moldy beets!**

I don't know what **mold** is, nor do I know how to turn a zombie
into anything besides smoke, but if that's what she wants to learn from
me, I swear **to Notch I'll manage somehow!!**

That's what I was thinking. Yet **a real warrior** wouldn't freak out in
such a situation, oh no.

Like the ice cream in my hand, a warrior's mind should be **cool and
calm,** sheer perfection crafted with the most skillful of hands—hands as
strong and supple as spider string, forged through countless hours of practice
and countless failures—hands that toss aside each imperfect cone until, at
last, a legendary-tier item is created, as flawless and smooth as diamond,
its icy depths containing a hidden power ready to be harnessed, savored—**a
power that is both minty fresh and able to change the world.**

Um.
Yeah.

My mind should be like that.

So, I merely looked at Nessa **in a bored way.**

"**Hurmm,**" I said. "Yes, yes, I see. **Hurmm. Most interesting.**"

"Well? What do you say, Runt? Do you think I have what it takes?"

What is she talking about? I gave her a **blank look,** like a skeleton spawning on a deserted island five sand blocks in size. She leaned forward in her acacia **stair block/chair,** leaned over the fence/carpet table. Once more, **Ms. Noob was smiling** so much that her eyes were like little moons.

"I, **Nessa Diamondcube, would like to join your team!**" She tilted her head slightly. Her smile somehow grew. "My friends call me **Lola,** though! **That's my nickname!**"

Join.

My.

<u>Team . . . ?</u>

"Whaat."

Notice the unusual spelling, here. Notice the lack of a question mark. It wasn't a standard "**What?**" or an excited/shocked "**What?!**"

Although similar to **the flat sound made by a sheep,** it meant much more than simply "**I don't understand,**" or even "**I can't believe what I just heard.**" It meant, "*Please place a dirt block above my head, because I'm about to jump so high I'll go past the sky, and if there's bedrock up there, I'll have gained so much momentum that I'll break through it, and I'll then travel through the void at faster than me-opening-presents speed—which is so fast that I'll be able to ignore the damage normally inflicted by this dimension, and that would be cool* since I'd go down in history as the first villager to explore that place, but I'd be without food, which would conflict with my previous goal of being the first villager to eat one hundred cookies in a single sitting."

Yes! I thought. *Yes, yes, yes! Of course, you can join! You can join us like two damaged swords merging together during the repair process!*

WOW, I'm **freaking out** again. I really have to stop that. Okay. Arctic biome. Arctic biome. I am the frozen, windswept plains.

I cleared my throat.

"Yeah. Sure. **I guess you can join."** A little shrug, real casual. "Yeah. Huh. Why not?"

"I can't believe this!" She sniffled. **"Thank you!"** She was so happy, **she was actually fighting back tears.** "Sorry, I'm just . . ."

"Yeah, uh, **don't mention it."**

(To be honest, I wanted to cry, too. And when I say cry, I mean create a new type of material known as the tear block.)

"One more condition," she said. "We have to hang out every single day!"

"Uh, sure. Okay."

"Great! We're going to have so much fun!"

I don't understand **why** she wants to hang out with me so much. That's part of the deal, though. **It might be hard.** I'm not used to being with someone so . . . **cheerful.**

It's going to be even harder training her. **I've seen her at the archery range.** I've seen her use a bow. Remember when Breeze **aimed poorly** on purpose? That's Nessa *(err, Lola, I mean. How confusing.)* on a good day, trying her absolute best.

I'm not trying to **be mean** or anything, just stating the truth. To date, she hasn't participated in a **single battle.** Unless you count hiding on the sidelines . . .

So even if I train her, her scores won't increase that much. Oh, well. If that's what she wants, that's what she's going to get, so long as it means her carrying us through **that test!**

It's official, then.
I've **welcomed** her aboard.
How could I not?
With this girl on our side,
Team Runt simply <u>cannot lose</u>!

Nessa/Lola talked for what seemed like forever. Then **Cogboggle** and **Block** walked into the garage. When they saw Lola and I chatting, they looked as if they'd just taken **five hearts' worth of damage.** They quickly recovered, however—and totally ignored me.

"Hey, Lola!" Cogboggle said, all smiles. "How's it going?"

Block spread out his arms and approached with the hugest grin. "It's **been such a long time!**"

"Yes, indeed it has!" Lola said. "I haven't heard from either of you since I **helped you with the last test!**"

"Sorry for that," Cogboggle said, following his friend inside. "We've **been really busy.** But we're not busy now, and we were wondering if you wanted to have a . . . **little chat.**"

"We just want to"—Block eyed me **suspiciously,** then smiled at Lola again—"discuss some things."

"Actually, I'm a little busy right now," she said. "**Sorry!** I've just had an amazing idea for something I've **been working on,** so I'll be heading home!"

"Hey, wait! We—"

"Let's talk tomorrow, **okay?**"

She waved and bolted **out of the garage.** I looked at the two of them and simply shrugged.

They glared at me. Moments later, they left the garage as well, stopping just outside. It looked like they were talking about something.

So I crouched and **began sneaking up to them.** I was still inside, hiding behind the wall near the edge of the door. It was **close enough** to catch their conversation.

This suit isn't just for show. I really *am* a ninja.

"Looks like he beat us to her," Cogboggle said. "I can't believe that little punk!"

"Maybe **she blew him off,** too?"

"Maybe. But if we find out she is working with him, **we'll have to do something about it."**

"I have something in mind, actually. **Let's go talk to the others."**

They ran off after that.

So those guys want her to help them, I thought. **What luck!** I found her at the perfect time!

When they were out of sight, away I went. I must have left **dust clouds** behind as I zoomed through the streets. I quickly forgot about Cogboggle.

Then I went to Stump's house and told him **all about what had happened.** "Dude, we've got **a redstone genius! A redstone genius! A redstone genius!**"

I talked to him so much about **Lola** that he got bored and started reading my diary.

"Dude," he said, "you've been writing an awful lot lately. Yesterday and today **are, like, fifty pages each!**"

"I write a lot when I get **sad.**"

"Look, you need to take a break," he said. "Come on, **let's go fishing.** I ran into Emerald earlier. She said she was going to the lake with her father and a bunch of humans."

Hurrr!

He's right.

I've been writing way too much these past few days, and throwing in way **too many details.**

If I keep doing it like this, soon my diary is going to contain every event that ever happened in the village

Every event. I said **this.** She said **that.** I was **angry.** She was **happy.** A pig **wandered into the village!** The pig **looked around!** The pig **oinked!** The pig **ate a carrot** that I fed him and both of us became super best friends! The pig is happy! Update—the pig **left! Where is the pig going?!** Why did the pig **leave?!** Why, Oinky, **why?!**

Fine, there's way more stuff to record, like that cloud over there! Yes, a cloud—above my house—**moved!** Get over here, cloud, and prepare to get recorded! Okay, it's moving eastward, I would say, with a speed of roughly **5.7 blocks per second.**

Sorry.

Okay, I won't write any more today. **I'm going fishing.**

Hurrr! Why didn't I at least take
Pebble's enchanted fishing rod?!
What's that Dredge enchantment?!

I'm at the lake, now. I was fishing with Emerald, Stump, Kolbert, Alex, Trevor3419 . . .

Then that old blacksmith, **Leaf,** sat down next to me. He asked if I could show him how to use a fishing rod. I didn't mention this before, but .

. . **back during the battle,** Leaf tried to help out. He was standing behind the front line, **fishing rod in hand.** He kept sending lures overhead, **snagging zombies randomly.** It did a little bit of damage. It also interrupted their movement slightly.

Sadly, Leaf didn't even know how to use a fishing rod very well, so he sometimes caught villagers and humans on accident.

I remember when his lure had snagged Emerald.

"S-sorry!" Leaf had called out.

Emerald had glared at him. "Hurmph! Maybe you should try aiming that **at yourself** next time!"

Then, **inspired by Leaf,** a little villager boy joined the battle with his own fishing rod. That kid snagged a zombie once, and he reeled it in **as hard as he could,** like he'd just caught a diamond or something.

The zombie flew into Razberry, who was totally confused. Razberry knocked the zombie back with his sword, but the mob flew right back in his face.

"So they can fly now?!"

Good times.

Okay, I know I said **I wouldn't write anything more today,** but . . . The **cloud that was over Stump's house** earlier is now over the lake. **It's a big cloud,** and dark like a rain cloud. Only, it hasn't rained at all. In addition, the cloud lit up a couple of minutes ago, as if from lightning.

However, there hasn't been any thunder.

At one point, the cloud flashed again.

"**Such strange weather,**" I said, sending out my lure again.

Leaf laughed. "Yew think that's a storm over there? **No! That's them! Fightin'!**"

"Who?"

"**The Gods!** Who else?"

After he said that, I stared at the sky for the longest time. Once more, the cloud flickered and sometimes lit up brilliantly **with streaks of red, violet, or blue.**

A lot of people **noticed it,** then. Villagers and humans alike **dropped their fishing rods** and stared up at the strange and colorful display.

Were Notch and Herobrine **really up there,** battling it out? Have they been dueling ever since they first clashed in our village? **How long will they continue? A cold wind** picked up. I saw Emerald draw closer to Kolbert. She looked **scared.** As the rest of us headed home, Emerald remained at the lake with the humans, **watching the cloud in silence.**

The cloud is gone. It drifted away just like any other cloud.

On my way back home, I heard a lot of villagers talking about it.

People are **spooked**.

Anyway, I don't have time to think about that.

My rivals are just a level behind me.

I have to study.

Time to crack open this **redstone** book.

This morning I woke up in bed, **facedown** in the redstone book. Last night I'd made it to the **third page.** In my defense, well . . . I'll just include a picture to help you understand.

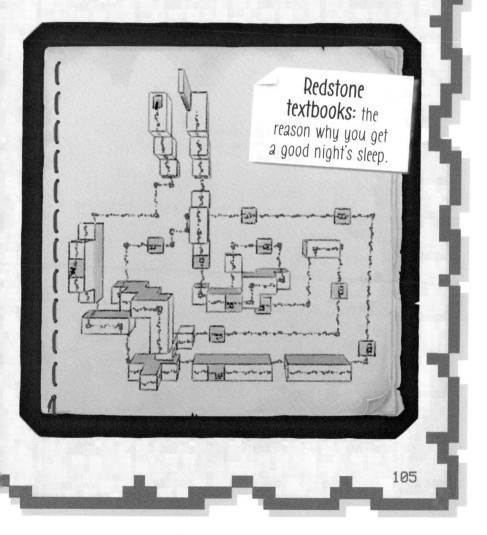

Redstone textbooks: the reason why you get a good night's sleep.

I sat up in bed and pushed the book away. **A lot** of stuff is going on right now. A *lot* of stuff. Herobrine is out there somewhere, amassing **a big army.** Then you have the humans who **showed up,** arguing with one another.

Pebble goes all "Urf" on us and gets **kicked out of the village.** Meanwhile, that crazy Brio keeps piling on the tests.

And any moment, Herobrine's mobs—which may or may not include **zombie/iron golem/cow hybrids**—could come knocking on our door.

 Yawn. A totally **normal Monday, then.**

Better get up and craft some tea and cookies. Well, no. I don't know where Mom **stashed the cocoa beans.** I threw some **wheat** onto the crafting table. Moments later, I wolfed down some bread and chugged a bucket of milk. *(I went back into my room and gave a loaf to Jello. He ate that thing faster than I did. The nerve! How could he show me up like that? Someday, we need to have a competition.)*

Of course, I would have asked my mom to craft breakfast for me, but my parents were still sound asleep. They've been **working harder** and harder in the fields . . . *They work so hard for our family and never complain,* I thought. **They're the real heroes. Not me.**

I went out into the gloomy, **rain-filled streets.** The black-robed guys could be found snooping around everywhere. Peering down wells. Creeping through farmland. Searching through villagers' inventories—even stopping the elderly and babies.

School today was the same way. You enter, you get **searched.** Use your inventory too much, you get **searched.** And if you're carrying anything **out of the ordinary,** Notch help you. Stump was one such person. Yesterday he'd crafted some new cookies. He added some stuff to the recipe to make a totally new item. Well, Brio's men spotted those cookies and dragged Stump away to a small, dark room. They **questioned him** for hours in there.

And when he finally returned, he looked **traumatized.** You see, after the questions, they did something horrible to my pal, something **unimaginable, unspeakable.** They . . . **took away** the cookies. Yes, in the interest of village security, the guys in black confiscated **my best friend's food invention.** After all, maybe Stump had added **gunpowder** to the recipe? **They didn't know.**

What a morning. I **couldn't focus** in Brewing II at all. Ms. Sugarcane just kept rambling. We're **low on Nether wart** anyway, so we can't brew much these days. *(Yes, we have a Nether wart farm. How do you think we've been crafting potions all this time? It's really small, though. We only have three blocks of soul sand. More on that later.)*

107

I spaced out and recalled my **meeting with Lola** yesterday. Sadly, she didn't show up at school this morning. *She probably skipped class to work on her machine,* I thought. And quietly, like a whisper in my mind, came another thought: *Redstone genius.* My mood **immediately lightened.** Classes flew by. During lunch, I showed my friends the last few entries of my diary.

"**Interesting,**" Emerald said. "I don't know if we can train her, **but we'd better try.**"

"It's not **possible,**" Breeze said. "She couldn't hit the broadside of an enderdragon from half a block away. No amount of training can fix that."

(Weird. That doesn't sound like Breeze. For some reason, she seemed irritated after she read my diary.)

I glanced over at Max to see what he thought. **He had his nose in a book.** When I looked at the cover, I cringed. *Village Law.* Again.

"Well, I **like her,**" Stump said. "I mean, I was a **noob** once, too."

Emerald shrugged. "She might be one slip away from stealing the **Noob of the Year** award from Bumbi, but . . . in a way, she is kinda smart, y'know?"

"Quiet down," I whispered, nodding at **the double doors.** "Looks like she finally **showed up.**"

Lola had just entered the lunchroom. She waved at us. Stump and I waved back. A hush fell over the table as **Lola approached.**

"**Hey, Runt!** These are your friends, right? **Hi!** Oh. Is it okay if I **join you guys?**"

When she said that, it almost felt like we were **the cool kids.** We're not, really, but it felt that way for a second.

Then again, a lot of kids **look up to Breeze** now. They don't talk to her much, but at least they **respect** her . . . or **fear** her.

The same could be said for Max. He's always been somewhat **popular.** Plus, Emerald is still arguably the **most popular** girl in school. Although I can't understand why.

And then there's Stump. Like me, **he's come a long way** from his noobly origins. After staring at Lola, he patted the row of seats. **A true gentleman.** She sat down next to him. "I heard about what happened in Brewing II. **Is everything okay?**"

"Yeah, no one got hurt," Stump said, "but I still **feel bad** for laughing like I did. I couldn't help it. The look on **Ms. Sugarcane's** face when her potion blew up . . ."

"One of your potions **blew up,** too," Max said, never taking his eyes off his book.

Stump blushed. What can I say? **He still has a ways to go . . .**

Anyway, Lola hanging out with us isn't such a bad thing. Even if she wasn't so talented with redstone, we could still use someone like her.

Someone **cheerful. Optimistic.** Forever upbeat. Max can be **negative** at times. Breeze, **withdrawn.** Stump, **mopey.** As for Emerald, well, she's all **over the place.** And I typically **whine** and **rage.**

I'm not sure why, but a **cheerful villager** is a rarity. We're moody. Maybe it's because of all the monsters attacking us over the years. We've endured a lot. So my friends took a liking to our team's **newest addition.** Here's the thing, though. **A few other kids took a liking to her, too.**

Just minutes after Lola sat down, **Cogboggle** and **Block** came over.

"**Hey, Lola,**" Cogboggle said. "**Are you still busy?** We've been wanting to chat."

Block made **a sad face.** "Yeah, **hurrr.** It's been weeks since we've hung out. **Why have you been ignoring us?**"

Maybe you can guess Lola's response: "**Me?** Ignore you? You must be thinking of someone else! Anyway, I'd love to **catch up with you guys!**"

(Facepalm.)

"**Great,**" Cogboggle said. "How about we meet up after class?"

Emerald shot up and wrapped her arm around our new friend. "Sorry, boys. She already agreed **to hang out with me** today!"

110

Lola blinked. "Huh? Did I?"

"Funny," Block said, smirking. "I didn't know you two were friends."

"Yeah, **well, we are,**" Emerald snapped, and gave him a look that said, *Back off, this is OUR redstone genius.* Then she squeezed Lola and smiled at her. "Isn't that right?"

"Yeah, um, of course!" ^^

Remember how I said Emerald is the **most popular girl** in school? **I take that back.** I **really, really** take that back. Apparently, **that title now goes to Lola.**

After seeing her sitting down with **Team Runt,** every other student realized what we were up to.

Everyone had forgotten about her. I only remembered her after running into her yesterday at the garage. It took us being seen together for that to finally **click** in everyone's heads. And the redstone connection was made.

Suddenly, everyone in school has become **Lola's best friend.** Everyone. **Even Bumbi,** whose life goal is . . . not graduating last.

By the time school was out, she'd become **a superstar.** She left her last class, books bundled in her arms, and kids swarmed around her like cows around the **Overworld's last wheat crop.**

"Hey, Lola, I was just **thinking** about you!"

"**Hurrr!** I brought you a gift!"

"How **long** has it been?"

"You look **so good** in those robes!"

"**I'm your BFF,** remember? Yeah, you remember!"

"Hey! I'm her best friend! **Not you!**"

"Lola, don't listen to any of these guys! I'm the one you want to hang out with! **Me!**"

"Lola, dear, **my bestest best-best friend,** you didn't forget about that favor you owe me, did you?"

Others were a bit more direct:

"We were wondering if you wanted to work with us on a project for the upcoming redstone test. **We're willing to pay. Handsomely.**"

This sparked a huge frenzy of offers:

"Look at my inventory! Anything you want, just take it, **take it!**"

"Carry me through that redstone test and I'll get you through **all the rest!**"

Others had no idea what was going on:

"Who is that girl? Whoever she is, **she's really cute!**"

"Is she a **new student** or what?! Why have I never noticed her before?!"

It was the first time Lola was **anything other than totally upbeat.** She was still smiling, but it was the kind of smile someone makes after hearing **a bad joke.** It was time to act. Team Runt formed **a shield** around her like zombies protecting **a creeper.**

Stump stood in front, ready to take a wither's fireball for his new friend. "Back off, **noobs! She's with us!**"

Their cries only grew louder, their movements more frantic. They tripped over one another as they tried **to hand Lola items,** anything from diamonds to enchanted books. Then I felt a hand on my shoulder. It was Cogboggle. **He shoved me. Hard.** I staggered back and slammed into this kid named Bubbles. Unfortunately, Bubbles was carrying a stack of emeralds in his arms. Those green gemstones went everywhere, and the sounds they made as they hit the cobblestone floor . . . it was like a creeper blowing up a glass house or something. Everyone turned to the three of us.

After that, they just stared **in total silence.** *(Well, an emerald had somehow landed on top of a sign. It finally fell down, causing a tiny bit of noise that echoed down the hall. Tink, tink, tink.)*

Bubbles looked like he was about to, um . . . **burst?**

Cogboggle was glaring at me.

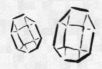

"Hurrr! I won't let this slide, Runt! She's **our** friend, **not yours!**"

His friends lined up on either side of him.

Block, Porcupine, Twinkle, Soulsand . . . even **Sara,** since Team Pebble was gone.

"**Everyone calm down,**" Max said. "I think Lola can choose her own friends, right?"

Block looked at her pleadingly. "**Come on, Lola.** Remember the fun times we had? **We made our first circuit together!**"

Lola flashed him a smile so bright, it was like everyone else was staring into the sun.

"Yeah, I remember! **That was great,** I have to say!"

"It was." Block returned her smile with one of his own. "So, why don't we work on another? **We're old buddies!**"

"**Sorry.** I'm afraid I'll be busy until after graduation," she said, "as I've agreed to **work with Runt** here! But after that, certainly! Why not?"

Boom.
<u>Boom.</u>

Although most here already knew that, her **confirmation** didn't help any. The rage, man. The rage. Kids started **freaking out,** shouting, shoving, and promising Lola the kind of **loot** only found in dungeons. Cogboggle and Block were **so mad** that they grabbed me and stuffed me into **a nearby school chest.** Judging by the items inside, I'm guessing it was **Bumbi's.**

Who else would use such nooberly items? That kid has no shame! I kinda like those dyed-green leather pants, though.

"**Seriously,** what are you guys doing?" I called out, my voice echoing. "This isn't a **double chest!** I can't fit in here! If you're gonna try to stuff me into a chest, at least do it right, **noobs!**"

Yeah, at least Pebble would have tried throwing me into a double chest. These guys, man. **Total amateurs!**

My friends came to the **rescue** by shoving Block and Cogboggle away. Stump pulled me out by my boots.

"**Get me out of here,**" Lola whispered to us. Her uneasy smile was returning. "I don't want any part of this!"

"**Sure thing,**" Emerald whispered. "We can hang out at my place. They won't be able to bother us there. **Trust me.**"

Breeze slipped Emerald and Lola **potions of Swiftness II.** "We'll see you there later," she whispered to Emerald. She looked at Lola. "Chug."

Lola wasn't about to ask any questions. She chugged, Emerald chugged, and they were gone faster than a cake in Stump's skillful hands. The crowd chased after them **like wolves after rabbits.**

Soon, the halls of the school were quiet again. **And empty, mostly.**

"My last two swiftness potions," Breeze said. She shrugged. "Worth it."

"Totally worth it," Stump said. "That poor girl looked **like a noob exploring the End!**"

Just then, I noticed a few teachers standing farther down the hall, **observing us,** as if taking notes.

Max spotted them, too. "Wonder why none of them bothered to break everything up? Kinda strange, no?"

"My father probably told them not to," Breeze said. "Didn't you guys notice? He was watching the whole time. **He can be a real jerk sometimes.**"

Sure enough, Brio was there, behind the other teachers, arms behind his back as always, eyes hidden behind black sunglasses, with **the biggest smirk on his face.** He approached. His **obsidian boots** tapped slowly and ominously against the newly placed cobblestone floor.

"I'd like to ask you something," he said, clearly looking at me. "It seems you've made **a new** friend, yes?"

"Well, um, yes." I swallowed nervously. "Yes. **Yes, I have.**"

He removed his sunglasses. His eyes are **different** from his daughter's, although similar in color.

117

When Breeze looks at you, you're reminded of the **soft glow of a low-level enchantment.** Brio's eyes are more like an enderman's.

"You've befriended her because you like her as a person," he said, "not for any . . . **other reason,** such as . . . personal gain. **Is that right?**"

Oh, man.
Why is he asking this?
Well, he's smart. Surely he knows what's going on here.

But then, once I **got to know Lola** more, I actually had started to like her. She's bubblier than a noob mining underwater until his air runs out, **sure,** but at the same time, she's a breath of fresh air in a school full of angry, **competitive kids.**

"**She's my friend,**" I said. "We met at the **garage,** she asked if I needed help, and before I knew it, I realized she's actually a **pretty cool person.** Her skill with redstone is **just a bonus.**"

"Very well," Brio said. "But there's something **you should know,** and I'll only say this once. **Everything has a price.**"

He threw his shades back on and let me **contemplate** what he'd just said. Then he smiled at us, particularly Breeze, and headed back to the other teachers, **whistling** a little tune.

118

"What was that?" Stump said. "Everything has a price'? What does that even mean? Could your father have been a little less vague?"

Breeze looked annoyed. "Dad's weird like that. Those cryptic warnings of his . . . I've heard them all my life."

"Then you must know what he meant," I said. "Are we going to get into trouble or something?"

She shrugged. "Don't know, don't care. We'll handle things as they come."

"By the way," Stump said, nudging Breeze, "did you ask him about how he was wielding two swords the other day?"

"No."

"Well, ask him! That was totally cool! I wanna learn how to do that! And where'd he get those obsidian boots?!"

Breeze rolled her eyes and sighed.
Hurmm.

So, Breeze seemed irritated today. Especially with her father. Yesterday, she said she had to go speak with him about something. I wonder what they talked about. Maybe he didn't agree with something she'd said?

Hurmm, **hurmm**, hurmm.
Once again, <u>Detective Runt</u> is on the job!

By the way, **Detective Razberry** has already gathered some nice
information.

OPERATION SNOOP:
REPORT

BREEZE	109
RUNT	106
EMERALD	104
COGBOGGLE	102
OPHELIA	101
BLOCK	99
MAX	97
SOULSAND	96
PORCUPINE	94
TWINKLE	92

Breeze and I are **still at the top.** Looks like Cogboggle really is
catching up to me, though. How'd he level up so fast?! **I don't know
much about Ophelia.** She's **polite** yet strong-minded and very
talented. A **model student.**

She wants to become a captain so she and her friends don't have to group up with someone like Cogboggle. She's kind of like the leader of this group of girls. **Team All Girls,** as I call them. They're mostly into **crafting** and **farming.**

Okay, I have to **stop** for now. Stump is **annoyed** at me because I've been taking too long with this entry. We're still at the school, and he wants to head over to **Emerald's house.** I've never been inside Emerald's house before.

I wonder what it's <u>like</u> . . .

"Good evening, Miss Emerald. **Guests?**"

Meet Charles. He's the head butler. As in, they have **multiple** butlers.

Wahhh**hhhh**!!!

That's the sound the giant zombie pigman made when he got blown up by TNT. It's also the sound a villager named Runt made upon viewing the inside of Emerald's house. **Quartz** columns. **Quartz** floors. Button-operated iron doors. **An indoor swimming pool.** And, of course, several nannies. The nannics craft breakfast, lunch, and dinner, do all the chest/item organization . . . and take care of Emerald's **baby brother, Pistachio.**

People actually **live like this?!** It's **not fair, man! It's so not fair!** I mean, I saw the outside of Emerald's house a long time ago. Her house looked big then, of course, but on the inside it's way, way bigger. We spent the rest of the evening chatting away in the **church-size chamber** Emerald calls her **bedroom**.

By the way, her bedroom has a bathroom. I wouldn't be surprised if her bathroom has a bathroom. And her bathroom's bathroom has another bathroom. And that bathroom has a bedroom, because dude, why not?

Every **now and then,** the butler came in to check on us, and offer us . . . refreshments.

Needless to say, **Stump took full advantage** of this. "**Ah,** hello, old chap. I've decided that I shall have another glass of melon juice before my nightly swim."

"Is that all, **Sir Stump?**"

"Hurmm. Now that you mention it, after my swim, my sword shall need some repairing, and my inventory shall need some tidying up."

"Of course, Sir Stump," he said with a slight bow.

Max was thrilled upon hearing that this house contains **a library.** With Emerald's permission, he went to go check it out. However, Breeze isn't **a big fan** of this place. She said the house, although beautiful, **felt cold. Clinical.** "Almost like **Herobrine's laboratory,**" she whispered to me.

Lola was, um, well . . . **Lola.** "**Thank you for inviting me!**" she said cheerfully. "It's so **nice** to have met such good friends!"

"It's nothing." Emerald stretched out across **the red wool sofa.** "If anything, we should be **thanking you.**"

"**Yeah,** Runt told us about how you offered to help us out," Stump said. "Strange how you guys just met like that, **right when we needed you.**"

Lola joined me over by the window.

"It's **not strange** at all," she said. "Even if we hadn't run into each other yesterday, I would have gone **looking for him.** I'd been wanting to **ask him** about this."

Breeze stepped between Lola and me. She glanced at me and then gazed out the window. "**Why him?**"

"Because he can **train** me! My combat score could use a little improvement, that's **no secret!** So I figured an exchange of knowledge would **benefit us both!**"

"An exchange of knowledge, huh." Breeze's voice was a little cold. "**So that's it?** He trains you, you hang with us, and you build your **flying machine** during the test?"

"**That's the plan!** Don't worry, we'll ace that thing! And someday, I'll even get it to fly in **more than one direction!**"

"**One direction?**" Emerald sat up on the sofa. "Wow. You mean, it, um . . . can't go **backward?**"

"It can. I just need **more time!**"

"It's not a **big deal,**" Stump said. "Flight alone would be better than anything else Cogboggle's crew comes up with, one directional or not."

Emerald smirked. "Not **arguing** with you there. That kid's a total blockhead. Well, I guess that settles it. **There's really no way we can lose now, huh?**"

We said a bunch of other stuff, but I can't remember it all. Some **stuff about Pebble.** I'm still in Emerald's bedroom, writing this entry while everyone else still chats away . . . **and eats diamonds. Just kidding.** Apparently, her parents don't have inventories **that** deep.

While I was about to finish up this entry, Stump asked the question that was probably on everyone's mind:

"Hey, can't your parents just give us a bunch of **diamonds? Enchanted swords?**"

"It's not like that," Emerald said. "We have a big house, but we're not **swimming in loot** or anything. Not anymore. **Blame the war.**"

"I don't understand," Stump said.

"Dude, it's a long story. **Long and boring.** Trust me. You don't want to hear it."

"If your family is so poor now, how do you guys have butlers?" Stump asked. "And security guards?"

"Some are from the group who **fled** from the other village. My father is the one who convinced the mayor to let them stay. They're just **repaying us,** I guess? Dude, I don't know."

"Oh."

Sigh. So no **free** diamonds, then. According to Emerald, **her parents have ten to their name.** Her allowance is even less than mine, too, which seems **hard to believe.** I'm really beginning to regret not taking all of Pebble's loot! **I want a diamond sword!** Well, maybe if I just mine up some of those **quartz blocks . . . I wonder how much they'd go for?**

Eventually, Max came back from the library. He didn't say a word when he came in. Something was bothering him. When I asked him about it, his face **grew dark.** "I guess now is as good a time as any."

He reached into his inventory and withdrew a **record book,** which he then placed upon a red wool stool. Like all record books, its surface gleamed brilliantly and held a **list of scores** below the student's name and level. Unlike most of our record books, some of the scores it displayed were **outlandish.**

Pebble's name was on the screen.

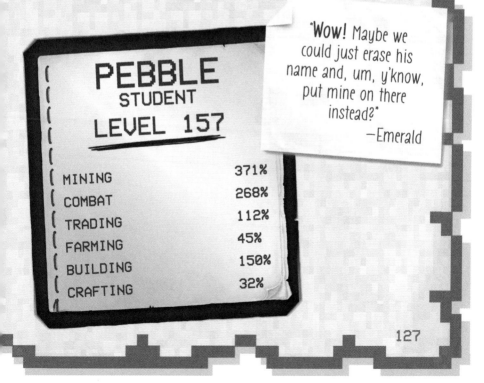

PEBBLE
STUDENT
LEVEL 157

MINING	371%
COMBAT	268%
TRADING	112%
FARMING	45%
BUILDING	150%
CRAFTING	32%

"Wow! Maybe we could just erase his name and, um, y'know, put mine on there instead?"
—Emerald

Before Pebble turned himself in, he'd **tossed his record book.**
Max had spotted it and secretly **tucked it into his inventory** when
no one was looking. How **incredible.** In the days leading up to his
banishment, Pebble had somehow retaken the lead.

This made me recall how serious he looked during training the past
few weeks. **Yet his mind had been <u>somewhere else.</u>**

So Pebble was some kind of **super guy,** huh? Hmm. I was only able to beat him because of my cloak's ridiculous buff. Once every full moon. I need to craft a calendar.

We **left** Emerald's house before sundown. Max and Stump walked Lola back to her place. I walked Breeze back to hers. **We chatted** on the way there.

"Do you think Pebble will **join Herobrine?**" she asked.

"How should I know?"

"Out of all of us, you've dealt with Pebble the **most.**"

I thought about this for a minute before answering. "I don't think he will, **no.**"

"Why not?"

"Because of what he said to me just before **he turned himself in,**" I said. "Although a bit crazy, it seemed he really did care about the village. **He thought I was a spy . . .**"

"What about Lola?" she asked. "What do you think about her?"

"She's cool in my book. How about you?"

"She's okay. I don't mind if she tags along. A little strange, though." She smiled and waved. "Have a good night."

"You,   too. **See ya tomorrow.**"

What's this? I thought. **No hug?** After glancing back at me **one last time,** Breeze waved again and slipped into her house. I couldn't see him, but I thought I felt Brio **watching me** from somewhere.

Everything has a price, I thought. **What did he mean by that?** I headed home. I felt **a chill** as the sun sank into the horizon.

These days, when you walk the streets this late, you'll notice some **houses without any doors.**

It's not a Building Fail, but the work of a paranoid villager. Some villagers now mine their doors away before sunset and replace them with blocks of stone.

TUESDAY

Today, school was worse than yesterday. In Crafting I, Soulsand told Lola he had a crush on her.

She laughed. "Don't joke around! You certainly can't be serious!"

"No! Really, I—" The school's note-block bell rang, cutting Soulsand off.

She waved and stepped out into the hall, where she was greeted by two more admirers. There was the flash of emeralds, and items formed a pile at her feet—as did Cogboggle and Block, who groveled on their knees.

"We really need help!" they said. "Please!"

"You guys are so silly! I'm not the only one who knows circuits, you know! What if I introduce you to some of my friends?"

"They're not as good as you! They don't even come close!"

"He's not kidding! When it comes to redstone, you make that Steve guy look noob!"

"I'm flattered! And really, I want to help you out! But it will have to wait until after I've completed my flying machine."

Still on their knees, Cogboggle and Block exchanged glances, faces filled with terror. Then they turned back to Lola and exclaimed simultaneously:

"Flying machine?!"

"Yes! Now, if you'll excuse me!" ^^. She made her way down the hall and found Stump and me. My two new rivals, as if stand-ins for Pebble, glared at me from afar with eyes of **smoldering lava.** Not that I'm worried. I'm not. I'm not. **I'm so not.**

Seriously,
what can they do? What?

Hurrr. It's pretty **dark** in here. So, this is what it's like to **be an item.** Who knew? Speaking of items, I wonder what's in here? Now, where'd I put **that torch?** . . . Figures.

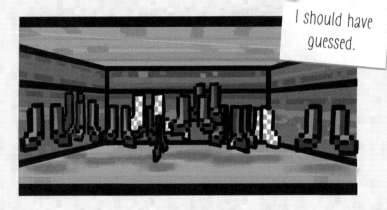

I should have guessed.

Man, what **rotten luck.**

It smells like a **pigman's feet** in here! You know, this is going to backfire on them someday. Maybe tomorrow they'll **shove me** into a chest with **lots of cool stuff.** Wait. They're talking. Their voices are muffled, though. Maybe if I just put my ear up against the . . .

"**Oh,** hi, Breeze. Um, nice to see you."

"**Runt?** Nope, haven't seen him. Wonder where he went?"

"**Us? Oh,** we're just checking this chest to, um, you know, make sure it's still, uh, sturdy."

133

"Yeah! Creepers can **blow up** chests pretty easily. Can't be **too careful** with so many of them running around."

"Hey, what are you—**OW! That really hurt!**"

"**Crazy girl!** Wait until your father hears about this! Whoa, calm down! **I'm sorry!** I'm sorry! I didn't mean it!"

"Dude, **let's get out of here!**"

. . .

Click.

"Just FYI, I'm still waiting for you to save me someday."

"Yeah. I'm waiting for that day, too. Believe me. This is starting to get embarrassing."

I climbed out. "Lola wants me to check out the machine after school today. **Wanna join us?**"

When I asked this, I could see slight **disappointment** in her eyes. She **bit** her lip, shook her head. "I told Emerald I'd go **mining** with her today. Another practice run."

"**Really?** Oh, okay. That's fine."

"Sorry."

"Yeah."

So they're preparing for tomorrow's test. **The test.** Max had heard that Pebble's family was going to **rig that test** somehow. Although Pebble's no longer around, I can't be sure his father won't try to **get revenge** . . . Of course, if Steve were still here, I'd zoom over to his place and ask for a tip—**a secret little strategy that only a human would know.** What about Kolbert? He's **certainly** been proving himself lately. He's so busy though, trying to get all the whiners **in shape.** A bunch of **pizza-loving crybabies** in iron armor! And some of the humans have formed **a new clan** called the **Creeper Crushers.** They're threatening to leave the village and go do their own thing.

All right.

I guess **that's that.** Time to go see what a flying machine looks like.

Our
top-secret
project.

A single slime block hung **in the air.** Around it, Lola placed two more to make a three-by-one-block row. She then connected **two sticky pistons** together, with a third on the opposing side. On this last piston, she placed a sign. Finally, she added **a layer of redstone blocks** on top of the green slime.

She wiped her forehead with the back of her hand. "Well, what do you think?"

"That's . . . it? **You're done?**"

"Yep. It might look simple, but it took me **weeks** to figure out!"

That's **a flying machine**? It looks more like a half-slime monster, half-redstone with piston arms . . .

START

Um.
I almost laughed.

If that thing's a flying machine, **then so am I.**

All you'd need to do is tell me we won't be having the mining test, and I'd **fly higher** than that thing ever could.

Then the worry set in. **The desperation.** It was now my turn to smile as if I'd just read one of **those ridiculous cow books.** "It's interesting, but . . . where are the **wings?**"

For the first time ever, **she looked slightly hurt.** She took out a stone pickaxe and began chopping at the sign.

"Wait!" I shouted. "Stop! I was just joking, huh?!"

She kept mining away. With one final swing, the sign broke away from the machine. Suddenly, the sticky pistons sprang to life, pushing and pulling the blocks of green ooze.

Clattering and clanging, the bizarre-looking machine began to fly through the garage, moving horizontally in the air. Its flight ceased when it hit the wall, although the pistons still whirred. Lola ran up, pick in hand, and mined away the three redstone power sources. The pistons stopped at once. Wow. It didn't look like much, but still. Today I saw a series of blocks actually move by themselves. The secret is in the slime blocks, Lola says. They have unique properties. They interact with sticky pistons in a special way.

"I'm still working on the **multidirectional version!** It will be **much better!**"

I glanced at the weird array of blocks. "Even in its current state, it's going to **blow away** the competition. No doubt there."

"**Wow!** You really think so?"

"Totally. We're going **to own** that test."

"**This is so great!**" She beamed. "After you become a captain, **we're going to go on all kinds of epic adventures!**"

When she said this, it was as if I'd been zapped by lightning. Her words echoed in my mind. *We're going to go on all kinds of epic adventures . . .*

EPIC
ADVENTURES.

WE.

. . .

. . .

Something was wrong. It hung in the air, **ominous, silent,** like gathering **storm clouds.** I couldn't quite understand what she was saying, although I sensed **the importance of her words,** felt the **horrible weight** they carried. I struggled to collect myself. I tried to grasp what she'd meant.

Meanwhile, Lola's smile **never wavered.**

"**Runt?** What's wrong? I thought you were going to become a captain!"

"Well, I . . . I **don't know about that,**" was all I could say.

"**You will,** of course. **I just know it!** And after graduation, **since we're now friends,** your group is where they'll place me!"

"W-what?"

"**Hey,** now! What's that face for? I thought you **already knew!** Cogboggle's a **real jerk!** As if I would join his group! No, there's **no other choice** but you!"

"Tell me—what are you saying?"

"Oh, come now, you really don't know? During graduation, the **Path of the Sword** is what I'll be choosing! I'm going to be a **warrior,** Runt! And you're **gonna be my captain!**"

Her words petrified me. In that moment, I became an **iron golem.** Made of metal. **Seemingly emotionless.**

A warrior. She wants to be . . . a warrior.

"As in, warrior **warrior?**" I trudged forward. "As in, swinging a sword, shooting arrows, taking lots of damage, and avoiding burning zombies as they try to hug you . . . **warrior?**"

She laughed. "**Uh,** don't be so dramatic! Who says warriors need to do all those things!"

Wow, I thought.
Is this girl **serious?**
She can't be! *She can't!*

Oh man, **what have I gotten myself into?!** For the past two days, I've been **dancing** on the clouds, and now . . . Since we're friends now, if I really do become a **captain,** they'll place her **with me . . . !!**

She doesn't know anything about fighting! Which means I'll have to look out for her. I'll be responsible for her!

"**Everything has a price.**" I get it now, you **crazy old noob!** That's what you meant! She might get me through that test, yeah—**but at what cost?!**

"I can't **agree** to this," I said. "You don't have much real-world experience, and—"

"You needn't worry, that's for sure! **I've been training every day!** I might've been a **noob** before, that's true! But I've improved a lot since you last saw me! Of that I can **surely promise!** ^^"

Her words didn't exactly fill me with **confidence.**

The last time I saw her training was but a week ago . . . She was in the yard, attacking a **dummy.** Her sword flew out of her hands in a way that would have made Urf so very, very proud.

"Show me your **record book,**" I said flatly.

"**Certainly!**"

NESSA
STUDENT
LEVEL 41

MINING	7%
COMBAT	5%
TRADING	1%
FARMING	17%
BUILDING	55%
CRAFTING	177%

Even with a crafting score like that, she still takes noob to a whole new level. At this point, even Bumbi is probably higher.

"See? **Already getting up there!**" ^^

"Yeah, um . . . I can see that. Still, I can't agree. It's for **your own safety.**"

"**Silly boy!** Don't joke with me! **You've already agreed!**" She clasped her hands together. "Oh, this is going to be so much fun! We're going to go on **so many exciting adventures!**"

"No, we're not!" I snapped. "You know, this is so unfair! I thought I was only going to train you! You didn't tell me about this!"

"I wanted you to train me because I didn't want to let you down!" She saluted me. "Warrior Lola of the First Scouting Group, reporting for duty!" Then she burst out laughing. "I sound so cool, huh? Oh, look at this map I crafted! It's mostly blank now, but just wait until we get out there!"

She's not only going to be a warrior, but she hopes to go scouting as well?! As in, she actually dreams of going out there? As in, beyond the safety of the wall?! As in, is she crazy?!

And the whole time, I'm going to be the one who has to babysit her! I'll have to watch her every move! And if anything happens to her, it'll be all my fault!

Arctic biome!
Arctic biome!!
Cool, crystalline ice!!
Crisp, refreshing air!!
Yeah, well, even places like that can have bubbling lava pools!!
HURRrrrgggggGGggggggggggggggggGGGgggggggggg!!

I didn't know how to **fix this situation.** So I avoided Lola today. **Or tried to.** Avoiding her was more or less **impossible.**

"I'll crush these guys with my machine!"

It's not that I don't like her. **I do. She's cool.** She means well. She makes me **laugh** sometimes.

It's just . . . I'm conflicted.
It's complicated.
Let me try to explain.

She's **bored with redstone.** She's going to become a warrior. Apparently, Stump and I had something to do with that. Back when school first started, Stump and I were **the definition of wimpy villagers.** The only thing we were good at then was eating cake. But **we had a dream.** We wanted to pick up swords and **defend** our homeland. So during those first few weeks of class, we tried our best. It was just as hard then as it is now, **sure.**

"Oh! It's not a double chest? No biggie. We can force you back in there."

And we **failed** just as much as we **succeeded. But we changed.** Grew **stronger.** During this time, Lola saw two noobs named Runt and Stump **skyrocket in level.** And she saw us befriend Max, who was considered one of the **smartest** students, then. She even saw me surpass Pebble in the rankings—a kid who everyone thought was **the best.**

A noble hero. Above all else, she heard of our **adventures.** Now she wants to do all those things, too. Even if it means experiencing **as much hardship** as us.

"Carroted"

(I'm here.)

She has a dream now. No one can talk her out of that. No matter what, she's going to open that chest, retrieve that sword, and hold it **proudly** above her head.

Later, she'll be assigned a **captain.** Drill said he will place **friends with friends,** which means she's going to be placed with me. She'll **endanger** our whole group! She could give away our position, do something **foolish** . . . I could be a **jerk,** I guess. Tell her to leave me alone. **Freak out in her face** until she **no longer wants** to be my friend. What then? **What would happen if I did that?**

She'd still pick up that sword. She would. The only difference would be that she'd be under **someone else's command.** Maybe **Cogboggle's.** Maybe **Block's.** Maybe **Soulsand's.**

If that happened, it wouldn't be **good news** for her. Many of the potential captains are almost as bad as Pebble . . . as I've recently discovered.

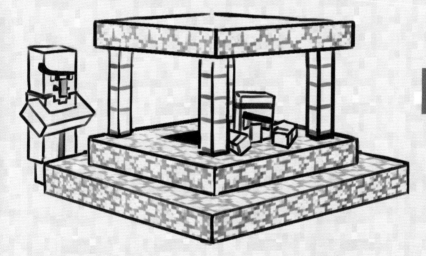

They'd boss her around. Treat her like a **slave.** Would make her go first into battle. Wouldn't care if she got hurt. If she was grouped up with one of them because I rejected her, how **guilty** would I feel? How could I sleep at night? Furthermore, if I ended **our friendship now,** she might get angry and let others use her design. If that happens, **I could fail** that redstone test. Maybe I wouldn't make captain.

Wow.
My head's starting to hurt again.
And I thought redstone circuits were complicated.
This is ten times worse.

Team Runt had lunch at the fountain. I told my friends about the situation with Lola. **I'm relieved now.** They don't think it's **that big of a deal.**

"I'll train her," Breeze said. "She won't turn into **Gogar the Destroyer** overnight, but she'll be **all right.**"

Stump: "Remember when we used to attack **grass** with sticks? **Who cares** if she's a noob! Let's give this girl **a chance!**"

Max: "Even if she's all but **useless** in combat, a redstone specialist could come in handy. Plus, from what you've said, she has the **highest crafting** score in school."

Emerald: "I say **we take her.** We can give her a bow and put her **super far back.** Then we can retrieve the arrows from the ground, wave, and shout 'Wow! **You're such an amazing shot!**'"

At about that time, I saw Lola **approach.** She had a **proud** look on her face, and she was carrying some strange-looking helmets. "Look what I **crafted!**" she called.

Lola then told us how she had discovered some **new crafting recipes.** The helmets in question looked like the helmets typically worn by miners. They come with a **special enchantmentlike** effect known as **Lamp.** It's almost like wearing a torch on your head. She also crafted human-style clothes for us, and enchanted each piece with **Fire Protection (I or II)** and the boots with **Feather Falling I.** Thanks to outfits like that, lava wouldn't be **as big of a problem** for us, and any falling damage would be greatly reduced. Not only that, but she dyed them bright **orange** for increased visibility in the dark. If we ever got separated, we could find one another easily.

"**Where's your outfit?**" Max asked.

"Oh, I didn't have **enough materials** to make my own set," Lola said. "But that's okay! **I made them for you guys!**"

"Aww, that's **really sweet** of you," Emerald said. She gave Lola a hug. "**Thanks a lot.**"

Stump gave me **a wink.** "You were saying?"

I raised my hands in defeat. What could I say? Here I was, **freaking out,** worrying for no reason at all. I just thought Lola might be a **hindrance. A liability.** More trouble than she's worth. Yet she'd crafted items that will **help us** out on the mining test. The hardest test to date.

Well, lunch is over. The test is about to begin.
We're going to go gear up. <u>Wish me **luck.**</u>

In these outfits, we almost **look like** humans. The girls have different pants. Lola said humans call them **shorts,** and human girls often wear them.

Humans, man. It's like they're **invading** our village. First, they charm us with their **wonderful ideas.** Then they talk about crafting their **mysterious** Earth food. Now some of us are even wearing their weird style of clothing? What next? **Maybe Kolbert will run for mayor?** Once someone discovers how to craft pizza, that's it . . . our village will no longer be the same!

These outfits are **kind of cool,** though. Dye the shirt and pants blue, and I'd almost look like Steve. We're also carrying **two pickaxes** each—*one iron, one gold*—along with a gold shovel.

Our iron pickaxes are enchanted with **Efficiency I or II,** meaning our arms will give out long before our tools do. As for the gold tools, well, they need no explanation. We've learned that there are situations in which such items can be useful. **Thanks, Kolbert.**

Then we have **buckets of milk and water,** stacks of **torches** and **food, potions of Healing I . . .**

In other words, we are **totally prepared.** The **ultimate** miners in all of Minertown. If someone trolls you by putting a block of stone in front of your door, just **call us;** we'll take care of it. We'll handle all your **mining-related problems.**

By the way, a few minutes ago, Cogboggle noticed our outfits and called us mining nerds. I think he's just **jealous.** But **it's weird**—he's **no longer being nice** to Lola. In the past hour, he hasn't talked to her at all. I wonder why?

Now we're just waiting for a few other kids to show up. As I write this, Brio and Drill are going on and on about basic safety techniques.

"**Good luck,** you lava splashers!"

"Be **careful!**"

"Careful? Oh, I'll be careful. I'll be careful to make sure I'm not the one going in first."
—Emerald

That's where the test will take place. The **shaft,** they call it. It's the main tunnel that the miners use.

We are actually going down into the mining tunnels. **How scary** is that, right? I can't help thinking about **Tunnel 67,** with its numerous warning signs . . .

As part of the test, some miners put **traps** down there. Nothing serious, I guess, but then, maybe Pebble's father set up some real nasty stuff, like lava. **Who knows?** There could also be cave spiders down there. They typically live in **abandoned mine shafts,** but maybe they're the reason mine shafts are abandoned in the first place. I mean, let's face it—if cave spiders mutated and started living aboveground, there would most likely be such a thing as an **abandoned Overworld.**

If someone saw a cave spider roaming around the plains beyond our wall, I'm pretty sure every last villager would pick up their things and **move to the Nether.** If the zombie pigmen kicked us out, **we'd move to the End.** And if the endermen kicked us out, well, I don't know what would happen, but I'm sure at least half of us would try **the void.**

Don't worry, though. I've already made sure my milk bucket is easily accessible. At the slightest squeak—**whoosh**—I'll swap to that bucket faster than a noob trading an emerald for a **blue-dyed egg** thinking it was a diamond. Yeah, anyone can swap items pretty fast. I have to say, though, I'm even faster than your average kid. While we waited,

I kept swapping between my pickaxe and milk bucket as fast as I could. Every time I did, I whistled, making a little sound—*phwew*—like a sword cutting through air. I did this for dramatic effect.

Phwew, milk! *Phwew*, pickaxe! *Phwew*, milk! *Phwew*, pickaxe! And then two swaps at once, super fast, so you could barely see the milk bucket I swapped to. *Phwew-phwew.*

Ninja speed, bro. **I'm not playing around.** No

cave spiders are **gonna get me!** 0.00001 seconds after those red eyes appear in the darkness, I'll chug this thing so fast that cave spider will think it actually spawned as a normal spider without **any poison at all!**

Emerald noticed me practicing this. "Dude. Why do you keep switching between your pickaxe and milk bucket? And . . . why are you making those sounds?"

"I'm just, uh, testing a . . . technique. Yes. **A technique.**"

She blinked a few times. "**Um,** whatever."

The rules of this test are pretty **simple,** by the way. The goal is to collect **fifty pieces of** . . . anything remotely valuable. That means any type of ore, including lapis lazuli and coal.

Okay, the last few students are here.
I'll update when I get back.

After the test began, each team flew down a **different tunnel.** Soon, the distant shouts and shrieks from the other groups faded away **completely.** We **walked** and **walked,** but there wasn't any ore to be found. The miners had really **picked** the tunnels clean.

Then our tunnel **ended** abruptly. Judging by the cobblestone, it had clearly been sealed off. A **sign** sat nearby.

DO NOT ENTER
TUNNEL 77B
RESERVED FOR
THE MINING TEST.

Stump **nudged** the sign with his foot. "Hey, **look at that!** There's something **written** on the back!"

Strangely, on the back of the sign was a single word, inscribed near the bottom.

BLOCKBIRD

(Yes, our world has birds. Kolbert freaked out when he first saw one. Blockbirds are basically fluffy blocks with wings. Imagine a chicken without a head—I think you've got the idea.)

"I think it's like **a code word**," I said. "**Miner slang.** Maybe it means **danger,** or maybe this tunnel is safe. **Pebble probably knew this language.**"

Stump looked around with **wide eyes.** "This place reminds me of **Tunnel 67!** I wonder if Pebble's father really did rig this place. But hey, maybe there's a lot of stuff down there!"

"I have a bad feeling," Breeze said. "Maybe we should try another tunnel."

"Are you kidding?" Emerald took a step toward the cobblestone. "We don't know what 'blockbird' means. This tunnel is just as good as any."

"She's right," Max said. "We can't waste time. I say we keep going."

"I know!" Lola said, beaming. "Let's do a vote!"

Yeah. Breeze and I were the only ones who voted to turn back. In the end, picks were swung, and the cobblestone wall gave way to . . .

a cave. It branched in two directions, so we agreed to split up.

"Why don't you go with Emerald and Lola?" Breeze suggested.

Then she gave me **a look** that said,
Make sure they don't do anything too noob, okay?

Shortly after we headed down the left branch, Emerald came up with all sorts of reasons for trailing **several blocks** behind Lola and me. At the same time, Lola went **full speed ahead,** all but skipping as she placed torch after torch. She just **wasn't afraid.** When a bat flew up to her, she caught it and **petted it** on the head.

Squeak, squeak.

"So **cute,** huh?"

"**Ew.** Gross." Then Emerald stopped and glanced at the wall. "Hey, **um . . .**"

"I think you need to enchant your glasses."
—Emerald

Wow, Lola really does take noob to a whole new level.

"I'll use my pickaxe to **mine** the ore!" Lola said.

Emerald and I exchanged glances. Our faces **were blank.** *Oh, you'll use a pickaxe to mine the ore?* I thought. *Are you sure? I thought you were going to use your forehead! Be right back—I'm going to go walk over here using my legs!*

We mined away **the entire coal vein** in silence, coming up with eight pieces of coal.

Then we **headed deeper and deeper** into the cave. I kept an eye on those two and listened for the **slightest noise.** We soon found another coal vein, and **Lola tore into it.** If it were possible to critically hit an ore block, she would have. As the coal dust settled, Emerald sneezed, which echoed through the cavern. After that, there were no more sounds. The three of us scanned the walls, which were bathed in the ruddy torchlight. We were completely alone, surrounded by crushing **silence** and countless blocks of stone, a **wall of darkness** just **ten blocks** up ahead.

Paranoia hung in the air along with a sense of **confinement,** of being **trapped.** At the same time, there was **freedom** here. Using our simple pickaxes, we could go anywhere we wanted.

There was even a sense of wonder and mystery as three hopeful miners **dug deep into the unknown.** This was the essence of mining.

Nothing captured this better than the sight of Emerald, panting slightly, pickaxe in hand, covered in coal dust, dirt, and sweat as she gazed into the cavern with eyes as bright as gemstones. **Even she'd gotten into the spirit.**

Miner Girl

"Come on," Lola said. "Maybe we'll find emeralds, and we can **trade them for new items!**"

"Trade them for new items?" Emerald called out from behind. "With emeralds? **Are you sure** that's what we use them for?! And here I was saving up for **a house on the beach!**"

Thirty minutes in, **we found a lot of stuff.** We were off to a pretty good start. We were doing **so good. So good.** I was doing good. Emerald was doing good. We were swinging our picks. We were making some progress. Then Lola really did find **some emeralds.**

"Too pretty, right, guys?"

Mmmmh, it's fishy.

Hmm. Something's off here. In a cave, you don't normally see walls like this. **It was too perfect, too flat,** as if **villager-made,** like the side of a house. And then there were those emeralds, just sitting there. It seemed too easy . . .

So I sensed **a trap of some kind.** A little surprise was waiting for us in that wall. Of course, Lola, being both **a noob** and a villager,

161

just couldn't resist one of the Overworld's **most precious** gemstones. Honestly, I wanted to mine those emeralds, too. They were just winking at us, tempting us. As I gazed at them, I **couldn't stop thinking about it.**

Come on, there's no danger in a little mining, they seemed to say. That's why you're down here, isn't it? A little swing here, a little swing there. Where's the **harm** in that?

I tried to **stop** her,
but it happened **so fast** . . .

Emeralds surrounded by a gravel wall . . . nah, it's not a trap.

"I'm on it, guys!"

Well, okay, **it was a trap,** actually.

Once that block **shattered . . .**

the gravel above fell down and water **splashed out.** A water block had been placed behind the gravel block, which created **an endless** torrent.

Normally, even this wouldn't have been all that bad. So my cookies get soggy. As if a little sogginess would stop me from eating them.

Unfortunately, this section of cave had a nice, steep slope. With a slope like that, the water could rush downhill. The current **took all of us**—and any nearby torches—with it. The water pulled us down and down this narrow tunnel until we hit a **waterfall.** And not just a waterfall: a waterfall leading nowhere.

Lola triggered the trap at the block of white wool. The water carried us to the block of obsidian.

It's called **a whirlpool trap.** I read about it once in Mob Defense class. Once the current dunks you, it's really hard to get un-dunked. So this section of cave had been modified. It had been engineered to accomplish this specifically! Pebble's father must have built this trap weeks or months ago. **Seriously,** is everyone in Pebble's family **crazy?!**

Just try to imagine this situation. **Just try.** One second, everything's going good. You've got ore. You're mining away. **You're happy.** The next, *boom.* You're swept away. **Totally without light.** Getting pulled down by the current. Taking gulps of air after being completely submerged. When you aren't submerged, some random bat is fluttering around in your face, squeaking and totally freaking out.

And during all of this, you don't know if monsters are going to spawn nearby to help you reenact a bizarre version of *20,000 Leagues Under the Overworld.*

UNDER THE SEАаᗅᗅa!
WATCH HIM BOOGIE!

(It's one of Pistachio's favorite village musicals.)

SWIMMING SO FREELY!
HAPPY ZOMBIE!

In first place for the test,
Team All Girls,
led by Ophelia!

In second place,
Team Zombiepunk,
led by Cogboggle!

OPERATION SNOOP:
REPORT

OPHELIA	116
COGBOGGLE	112
BREEZE	111
RUNT	108
BLOCK	108
EMERALD	106
SOULSAND	106
PORCUPINE	104
TWINKLE	102
MAX	99

*Cogboggle passed me!
I have to hold on to at
least fifth rank! This is
really, really bad . . .*

We had a little **mishap today. A little setback.** We got fifth place in the mining test. **How annoying.** At first, everyone was angry with Lola and even angrier at me. I'm such **a bad babysitter.** Moreover, I was the one who had **agreed** to let her hang out with us. But then Stump said it was their fault, too. After all, Breeze and Emerald could have taken Lola with them when **they went mining yesterday.**

"It's **our job** to look after her," he said. "To make sure she doesn't do anything **too noob.**"

So after school today, we all went out to the park with our **swords drawn.** With the **combat test** scheduled for tomorrow, we were going to turn Lola into an **efficient,** zombie-destroying machine. Or that was the theory. In practice, it didn't work out so well.

We spent hours training her, giving her all kinds of advice. She must have swung **her wooden sword** a thousand times. Somehow, her combat score didn't go up a single point.

"Oh! So this is the handle! Well, we all make mistakes, don't we?"

Noobishness runs in her blood, Breeze says. There's **no changing that.** Everyone has **strengths** and **weaknesses.** We just have to accept it. We wanted to practice throwing some snowballs, but we didn't have any. The mayor has a snow golem **locked up** somewhere that provides the snow.

Things are only **getting worse** as time goes on. One of the **reasons** Breeze has been acting **strange** is because of Lola. I realize that now. **Breeze denies it,** of course, because that's just how she is. She always hides herself. Rarely tells me how she's feeling. Still, I know she thinks **something is going on.**

"Hi, Runt! I bought you some cookies!"

Is something going on? Does Lola **like me in . . . that way?** I don't think so. We're just friends, nothing more. **Aren't we?**

   It's funny, you know? Out of all the challenges I've faced so far, this is **the most difficult yet.**

Dealing with monsters is easy compared to this. Grow a giant mushroom. **Dig a trench.** Or simply fire a bunch of arrows. That's it: **problem solved.** But this is **different.** It's too **complex.** There are no easy answers. It would have been so much easier if I'd never gotten to know her. I've felt that way since yesterday, and that feeling only grew stronger today during the first part of **the combat test.**

"Don't worry! I've been training a ton!"

"You're my best buds!"

When Lola had offered to **help me out,** I had been **blinded.** I only saw what I could gain and never really thought about what she could have wanted. I only saw her redstone **talent,** and I never considered the potential **downside** of letting her on my team.

"**Wow!** My sword flew
farther than my arrow!
Is that a special attack?"

As soon as I agreed to be her friend, **that was it.** She became **my** responsibility, my problem.

And now the first section of the combat test is over.

In less than fifteen minutes,

the Ice Cup tournament will begin.

171

Ice Cup is an **annual** event in my village. As I've mentioned, we play **Skyball** in this single-elimination tournament. Skyball is pretty simple. Each team has a **runner** who stays behind the stone wall on their team's platform. The runner's main job is **to avoid getting knocked into the water.** *(By the other team's snowballs.)* The rest of the team are **guards.** They stand in the front section of the platform. They must **protect the runner** from the opposing team's snowballs while hurling a few of their own. If a team's runner falls into the water below, **that's it. They lose the match.**

172

Guards

Runner

Sadly, Brio decided to **change** things up. "This year, I'll be choosing each team's runner," he said.

When he said this, I sensed that he was looking at me specifically. He was **smirking** at me.

Yeah. Who do you think he **chose to be our runner?** Who do you think he chose to be the single most important member on our Skyball team? **Who? Who?**

Lola, that's who. Brio kept **smirking** at me while the teams prepared themselves. He was **enjoying** this. But it's not so bad. We've been matched against a **really noob team** in the opening round. *That team features such legendary all-star greats as Bumbi and Bubbles.*

We'll just have to protect Lola, I guess. I'll **block** snowballs until I turn into **a snow golem,** if that's what it takes. We were each given potions of **Regeneration I.** Snowballs don't deal much damage, but I guess Brio just wants us to be safe. **Our match is about to begin, so . . .**

The match was intense.

As we found out, Bubbles is apparently **a Skyball master.** He might be **ranked 145th** in school, but up there on that platform, he was the king. That kid would jump and weave around in the air to fake us out, and he threw those snowballs **so hard** I swear they went faster than arrows.

This other kid, **Loaf**—well, he didn't do much, but he didn't have

to. He's one of the **biggest** kids in school *(over two blocks high and one and a half blocks wide).*

We were totally outmatched. After all, **Lola** was our runner . . . and Breeze had apparently **never thrown** a snowball in her entire life. Still, as long as we stood in front of **Lola,** we'd be okay.

Then Bubbles threw a snowball almost **straight up into the air.**
Lola wasn't moving around much, you see, and she certainly didn't notice
that snowball coming from **fifty blocks up.**

There was **no way** we could block that snowball.
She had to move. I wanted to **warn her,** of
course, but I took a snowball to the face just after
I opened my mouth. When I whirled around, I
took two more to the back of the head.
Just in time to see Lola
look up one second
before **the snowball
hit her face.**

Oops!
Sorry!

. . . last place goes to **Team Danger Kitty**, led by Runt.

Everyone's **angry** with me now.

OPERATION SNOOP:
REPORT

OPHELIA	135
COGBOGGLE	127
BLOCK	123
SOULSAND	121
PORCUPINE	119
TWINKLE	117
BREEZE	111
RUNT	108
EMERALD	106
MAX	99

Ophelia is pulling ahead of everyone **in the rankings.** She's the only one on her team with high-level scores. The rest are around **90%** now, I guess. She's carrying them. And then everyone in Cogboggle's **rotten crew** has passed us up. Breeze is in **seventh** place now, and I'm in **eighth.** One of us needs to be ranked at least **fifth** to become a captain.

I'm so angry that I can't even write. How is this happening? How did we lose to Team Noob in a **Skyball match?!** We got knocked out of the tournament in the first round! Why couldn't those noobs just let us win?!

I'm going to go
punch a tree.

Well, this is it. Lola might have cost us **two tests,** but she'll make up for it with this one. The redstone test is **why she's here.** Even though we fell behind, we'll more than catch up once she unveils her **masterpiece.** Once Brio sees that marvelous invention, his eyes will become **larger** than **enderpearls,** and Team Runt will bounce back to the top like a slime under the effects of **Leaping II,** bouncing on a slime block.

In front of everyone, Lola revealed her **flying machine.** The slime blocks. The redstone blocks. **The sticky pistons.** The sign. **People were amazed,** at first. Kolbert was here with Emerald, and he said Lola's invention reminded him of the **Industrial Revolution.**

"Do you know what this means?!" he said to Alex and Trevor3419. "This thing can **change the world!**"

"We'll begin working on it at once, **sir!**" Alex said.

Trevor3419 gave Kolbert a salute. "We'll put **our best men** on the job!"

Then it was **Team Zombiepunk's** turn to unveil their creation. I wonder what those noobs have come up with, I thought. Whatever it is, they won't beat us. One by one, Brio and several teachers removed the blocks of wool surrounding Team Zombiepunk's redstone creation. Can you guess what it was? **Can you?**

Yeah.
It was a flying machine.

With slime blocks, redstone blocks, **sticky pistons . . .**

They modified it just a little bit to make it look different, **of course.**
And **Team All Girls?** **Also a flying machine!**

In fact, pretty much every team had a flying machine!

Huh. Imagine that. Seems like everyone else had the **same idea.** How
odd. **How mysterious. How coincidental.**

I wonder how they all came up with a **similar design?** Cogboggle
and Block totally didn't spy on us when Lola built it in the garage . . .

Of course they did. They're not **dumb.** I'm the one who never even
thought to make sure she built her invention in a secret location . . .

We just got counter-snooped. I gained **some levels,** of course, but so
did everyone else, so the rankings are still the same.

It's over. It's all over. **My dreams are gone.** The final is on Monday.

I'm sure I'll manage to
<u>mess that up, too.</u>

I had **bad dreams** the whole night. In every scene, Lola was in **danger.**

"We're going to have so many fun adventures!"

"Poor little guy. I think he needs a hug."

All of this is happening because of **a single decision** I made. I was **selfish.** Greedy. Out for myself. And now **I'm being punished.** There's nothing I can do to fix this. Breeze is **angry** with me, and now I won't even make captain.

Fine.
I give up, okay?
I don't even want to be a warrior anymore . . .

I had the same **nightmares** tonight. They finally **subsided** and everything went black, until—

"It's been ages, **kid!**"

As if my dreams weren't **bad enough.** Now I get to listen to this **bonehead** talk in that scratchy, **gravelly** voice of his.

"Bonehead?!"

"I'm not the one who just bombed **three tests!** Hey, I'm sorry, all right? **Hey!** Don't shut me out, kid! Look, I'm not going to ask you to save me! **Someone else already did!** Don't look at them like that! **They're not monsters!**

183

Well, okay, they are monsters, and so am I, but we're good! **We're not like the rest!** We've made a whole city by ourselves! A city of good monsters, **hidden from all the bad ones!** By the way, this is Eeebs. He won't bite. Promise! Oh, and that's Clyde over there. Both of them are really nice!

"Okay, okay, I don't have much time. I just wanted to tell you . . . you think you know a lot, Runt, **but you really don't.** There's a huge world out there, kid. **You can't even imagine.** How could you, **stuck** in that tiny village? You haven't seen a thing!

"When you get a chance, you need to **go out there and explore!** Leave those walls! There's so much you need to learn! So much you need to see! Anyway, that's all I wanted to say. Visit me sometime! Ask around for **Batwing!** That's me! We're gearing up to fight that creepy guy with the glowing white eyes.

"One more thing, Runt . . .

"Even if you don't make captain, who cares? **You're already a warrior, kid!** What counts are your actions and what's inside of you, not a bunch of **silly** tests! Oh, don't look so confused. That Pebble kid might have been a little crazy, **but even he knew that!**"

I woke up covered in **cubes of sweat.**

Was it really just a dream? Or . . . was it real?

Well, Breeze has been dreaming the **exact same thing.** It seems hard to believe, but . . . maybe a monster is actually **communicating** with me.

That's strange though, because Breeze said endermen, not **wither skeletons, control dreams.** Maybe the skeleton was using a magical **item?** Max told me that some endermen are amazing crafters. Even **wizards.** I need to do more research with him. Anyway, I don't want to **leave the village.** How could I? **Batwing** can go bug Lola, and she can go to visit him, and the two of them can become **the bestest best-best friends.**

Does this mean Pebble is still alive?!
Not only is he still alive,
but he has a horse?!

The big day. I'm in the cafeteria. So is every other student. We've all been **working** on the final—writing down our ideas about how to get **revenge** against the mobs. By now, almost everyone has turned their paper in. We're just waiting for the teachers to review our submissions and determine the winners. They sure are taking their time. What's the holdup? As if it's **hard to decide.** We might have worded our papers differently, but the **general idea** is the same.

> I THINK
> WE SHOULD
> BURN THE MOBS'
> FOREST.
> -STUMP GOLDENFEATHER

In my opinion, the best way to take revenge would be: Start a fire in their forest. Wouldn't take much effort on our side, so it's a very effective way to disrupt their plans.

—BREEZE

STEP 1:
WALK UP TO THE FOREST

STEP 2:
USE LIGHTER

STEP 3:
GIVE ME AN A++

-EMERALD SHADOWGROUND

TREE

BUCKET

FIRE

(Yeah, I didn't try very hard. I've pretty much given up.)

LAVA

HOMELESS ZOMBIE

—RUNT IRONFURNACE

CUPCAKES ARE VERY HARD TO MAKE. YOU NEED SUGAR, BREAD, EGGS, MILK, AND FOOD COLORING. I LOVE CUPCAKES. IT'S COOL. EVERY DAY I WAKE UP AND WONDER HOW MANY I'LL BE ABLE TO EAT.

(This is Max's submission. He didn't put his name on it. Looks like he's given up more than I have.)

Of course, Lola is still hanging with us, **as cheerful as ever.** I've decided **to not get angry** with her. As I said, all of this is my fault. **(I don't need to point out that she was the last student to finish writing her paper . . .)**

"I've put **a lot** of thought into my idea!" she said to me. "I think it's really good! **Would you like to hear it?"**

"No, thanks," I said, not even glancing at her paper. I figured her idea probably involved talking with the mobs in a peaceful way. **Maybe some flowers.**

No, I wasn't **curious** in the least. **Neither were my friends.** Breeze didn't say a word to **Ms. Noob** the whole day. Well, **that's that.** BRB, diary—gotta go fail one last test. My life just won't be complete until I do.

Prepare for an update filled with rage,
and **crying,** and **whining,** and *hurgging,*
and **freaking out** in general.

Cake biome?!
Fermented pickaxe?!
Protection from Pumpkins V?!

Brain . . . malfunctioning.
Bzzzzt. **Bzt.** Bzzzzzt.
Bzt-bzt. . . .

Bzzzt.

P-potato . . . ?

I . . . I-like . . .

p-p . . . p . . . p-p-**ppotato?**

This is Breeze.

Runt is trying to write in his diary, but he **can't.** I suppose he is **too shocked** at what just happened. I could write about that in detail, but I have chosen not to. I am writing in here so he doesn't make any more **strange entries.**

Runt, when you read this . . . I am **sorry,** but I read some of your previous entries. It's true, I've been **jealous of Lola**. You two were spending so much time **together.** I hope you can forgive me. I've been acting childish. Again, **sorry.**

—**Breeze,** who wishes she
knew more about redstone . . .

It's Emerald.

Dude, Runt is like, totally **freaking out.** Honestly, I am, too. I mean, dude—what just happened? **I can't believe it!** Still, though, I'm not **freaking out** the way Runt is freaking out. He's been running laps around the combat yard for the past fifteen minutes and screaming the whole time!

Okay, yeah, um, sorry for writing in here. I saw Breeze doing it and thought it'd be kinda **fun** if I did, too.

Lola is **really cool,** by the way. I know that now. We're gonna go **trading** together as soon as we're not busy. And not just window trading, either. We're totally gonna go on the biggest **trading spree** ever! And she's gonna craft me this thing called a dress and these special boots called **sandals!**

Wow! I can't wait!
Some of that human-style clothing looks so
super, super cute!

Meow! Lola here! ^_____^

I'm letting you know that you left your diary in the cafeteria. Silly boy! Breeze, Emerald, and I have been writing stuff in here because it's **really neat! Wow!** I feel like a real warrior recording my thoughts and feelings! **So cool, right?**

And yes, I know I've made a few mistakes these past few days, but that's all part of the learning process, **isn't it?** Anyway, you should now know that I'm **not as noob** as you think! Don't worry, Runt! **We're going to do great things together!**

=<^.^>=

A happy kitty just for you!

~~XOXO, Lola~~

(PS, I don't know what XOXO means! I saw some humans writing that and thought it'd be cool to include!)

Dear diary,

Why does everyone keep writing in you? Is this the cool thing to do now? That's fine. I, Stump Goldenfeather, **am officially cool now.**

Yeah. So. Something **ridiculous** happened during the final. I was going to write about it since Runt can't, but Breeze and Emerald are telling me not to.

Hold on.
They're not looking.
Okay, so what happened is—

Runt,

For the record, I have taken your diary **away from Stump.** This is your diary. No one should be writing in here **except for you.**

I will say: **I am as shocked as you** are about what happened during the final.

-Max Whitecloud

Yeahhhhh!!
I stole Runt's diary!
I took it from that **noob**, Max!
I snatched it right out from under his big, blocky nose!

Then I ran through the school halls with it, waving it over my head! **What a rush!** This feels so great, just like that time I stole those **diamonds** from that human!

Oh, great. The **guys in black** are coming. So annoying. Those blockheads are always on my tail . . . What's **their problem**, anyway?! So what if I scammed that kid out of his emeralds the other day!?! That noob didn't need 'em! Time to show these guys why people call me **the sneakiest villager around!**

Until next time,

—**Cogboggle**, everyone's favorite villager

I'm hiding in the school **supply** room. **I totally gave 'em the slip!** Those cobbleheads walked right past me! All right, I gotta stash this book somewhere. Can't be **caught** with this thing in my inventory. **Oh, and just so you know,** Runt, you might've pulled ahead, but we still have to finish out **the final!** After you mess that up and none of you make captain, your whole crew is gonna be **shining my boots** to a diamond gleam! Especially that **annoying little Emerald!**

Warmest regards,

> —**Cogboggle,** the coolest/greatest/sneakiest villager of all time, and **dungeon-looter extraordinaire**

Uh . . . This is **Bumbi.** What is this diary doing in my inventory? Just to let everyone know, **I did not steal this book.** Since I'm writing in here, I'll just say that **I am really sad,** because I am now in last place. I'm rank **150** now. Even Lola is ahead of me. And **Bubbles.** Bubbles! This isn't good. I wonder if they will still let me be a warrior? Maybe I can join **Runt's team.**

Wait, is this Runt's diary? **Wow.** It is! **What luck!** Runt, if you read this, I want to know if I can join your group after we graduate. Pleeze let me know. **Plzplzplz.** I will try my best.

Oops. It looks like everyone took off to finish the final test. I need to be there.

This is Bumbi, by the way.
Bye.

Official notice:

This book has been confiscated by the school board. As this item has been modified to such a degree as to fall within the category of strange and unknown items, its threat to village security must be assessed. Furthermore, this item may contain potentially sensitive information, and as such, we cannot risk letting it fall into the hands of the enemy until its contents are deemed safe.

Upon its approval, it will be returned to its owner, Runt Ironfurnace.

—**Brio**, Administrator,
School of Minecraft and Warriory

Official notice:

Due to the extent of this item's modification, the review process is taking longer than usual. In addition, some entries appear to describe the mayor in a negative fashion, which could be harmful to his image as the brave leader of our village.

Therefore, the school board is now determining whether or not this item should be placed within a lava incinerator for its immediate destruction and its owner appropriately reprimanded.

—Slab, Administrative Assistant
(referred to in this diary as one of the "guys in black,"
"Brio's goons," "creepy weirdos," "thugs," or "blockheads")

211

Official notice:

I, the mayor, hereby declare my intention to designate "Villagetown" as the official name for our village.

Furthermore, I hereby decree that all entries within this diary that portray me in anything other than a stellar light are to be regarded as entirely fictional.

—The Mayor of Villagetown

I, Runt Ironfurnace, **officially** acknowledge that any part of this diary that suggests the mayor is a total noob just **isn't true.**

I also agree to **never write** any such imaginary events in the **future,** as they could tarnish the mayor's good name.

Lastly, I will spend Tuesday afternoon in the **school kitchen** crafting various **potato-based food items.**

—Runt Ironfurnace

Finally.
Finally!

Brio **gave my diary back to me.** The guys in black studied it for days to make sure its contents were "wholesome" and not a **"threat to village security."** Well, some of my entries do contain a lot of **top-secret** information, but there's no chance the mobs will get their hands on this book. I will eat every last page before that happens. I will. And I could do it, too, believe me. **I get really hungry sometimes.**

Well, enough of that! How about we go over what happened on Monday?! Just remembering it makes me **wanna f-f-freak out, man!**

Okay, so there we were, waiting in the cafeteria. **Lola was bugging me** about her idea, and I just brushed her off. Dude, all of **Team Runt** was fed up with her. And **fed up** with me. Even fed up with themselves! I mean, we came all this way, we studied and practiced and trained and took **all kinds of risks** to do well in school, and then this happens?! **Cogboggle, that punk!** He **stole** Lola's idea! He stole her idea and other kids found out about it, and suddenly **every team** had a flying machine.

I was sitting there, **thinking** along these lines. Then, before the entire school, the mayor held up a **stack** of papers. "We will now announce **the winner of the final test**," he said.

"**Unfortunately**, almost every entry was identical," Brio said, "resulting in a tie between every team. **Except one**."

A lot of students **groaned**. So almost everyone had the exact same idea?! **But it was a good idea!** How could the mayor not want to burn that forest down?! One time I saw a zombie standing underneath those trees with this **smug little look** on his face.

Oh, look at me, that zombie was probably thinking. *The sunlight can't touch me! We're so clever! We made a forest right next to this village where we can roam all day!*

No, **we had to burn it down!** There was no better way to get revenge. Yet apparently there was.

Whatever it was, it was something only the sneakiest villager would come up with. **No**, I thought. **No way! It can't be! It just can't be! It's not possible! Cogboggle's . . . going to win?!**

The mayor put away the stack and held up a single paper. "Yes, out of every submission we've reviewed, **only one stood out.** Well, there was one that said something about **cupcakes,** but there was no name, so . . . we threw it out."

He handed the paper to Brio, who shouted: "And the **winning submission** belongs to . . . **Nessa Diamondcube!!** Oh, it says to call you **Lola.** Sorry. Please come up, dear."

Boom!

The crowd **exploded** like a powder keg. *(That's an item Max read about in an ancient book—its blast is stronger than a charged creeper's.)*

Anyway, no one could believe it. **Lola won?!** How could a noob like her come up with such **an amazing idea?!**

With **a shriek,** Ms. Noob clutched her chest and bounced up and down like a slime who'd just consumed an entire stack of sugar. Then she made her way up and stood next to Brio with a smile **so bright** that if anyone here had been a zombie in disguise, they would have burst into flames.

"We really **loved** Ms. Diamondcube's idea," the mayor said. "It's so **elegant,** so **splendid** and **wonderful,** simply bursting with the kind of ingenuity we so desperately need . . ."

And when he said that, I suddenly **remembered** that I used to be like that. I used to be a noob just like her, trying so hard to prove myself. Back then, I never would have asked some stranger for help. Back then, I would have come up with **my own idea.** Have I become lazy? **Or am I just stressed out?**

Anyway, Lola finally pulled through.

OPERATION SNOOP:
REPORT

OPHELIA	137
COGBOGGLE	128
BLOCK	124
SOULSAND	122
PORCUPINE	120
BREEZE	119
TWINKLE	118
RUNT	116
EMERALD	114
MAX	107

And since she was on our team . . . That was the point when I totally freaked out.

Our ranks didn't change, I thought, *but we're only a few levels behind! If we do well on the second part of the final, Breeze and I can hit the top five! Even if I don't make captain, and Breeze does, that's enough for me! I'll salute her, craft her breakfast . . .*

I ran out of the cafeteria and started running laps around the combat yard, totally screaming at the top of my lungs. In that time, my friends wrote a bunch of stuff in my diary—along with Cogboggle, who wrote a bunch of nonsense. I'm the sneakiest villager, not him!

Thirty minutes later,
all 146 students began to carry
out the plan proposed in Lola's submission,
the title of which was . . .

WELCOME, MOBS,
TO SUPER HAPPY
FUN TOWN!

This village is both fun and super happy. Can you tell?

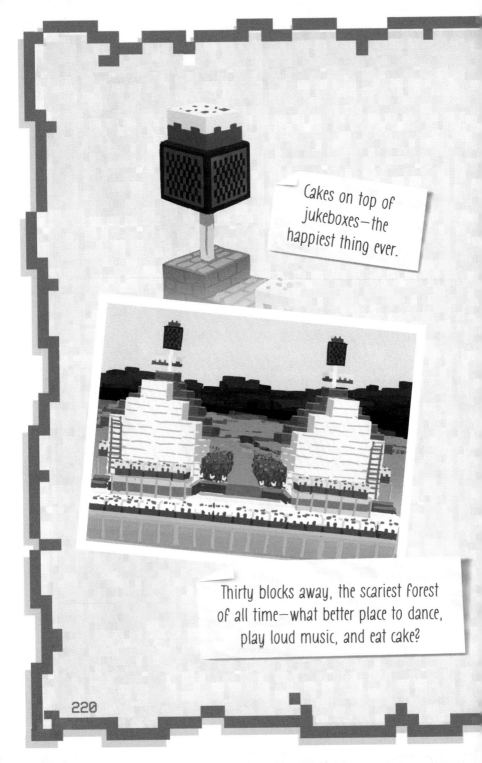

Cakes on top of jukeboxes—the happiest thing ever.

Thirty blocks away, the scariest forest of all time—what better place to dance, play loud music, and eat cake?

Yeah.

We built **a little party area.** So cozy, right? So cute, so lovely, so innocent and girly. But this **happy** little place, smelling of flowers and freshly crafted cake, **had a dark and terrible little secret.**

Hidden beneath all that frosting, beneath the pink glass blocks, the rose bushes, and the seastone lanterns . . .

was our version of Boom Mountain.

"A-a-**all** right, you guys place the TNT, and I-I-I'll just go wait over here. I mean, someone has to watch the forest, right?"
—Emerald

The **idea** went like this: We were to dance in **Super Happy Fun Town, laughing** and smiling and **joking.** The mobs, who hate **cute** little places like this and super-hate seeing villagers having fun, would rush out. We would then light one block of TNT just before the mobs entered, we'd run back, and the zombies would be given **a free one-way trip to the void.** *(I would then have my cup of tea.)*

And it went like that, **it did.** Emerald threw some music discs into the jukeboxes, and they started **blaring** away. Stump, Max, and a few others climbed up the ladders and did **some jigs** on top of the houses.

'I'm so happy!' Stump called out, arms and legs moving wildly. 'Good thing the mobs aren't attacking us! **We're having so much fun over here!'**

The rest started dancing down below.

Strangely, Lola still wasn't around—she **disappeared** right after we began building. So Breeze was **happy.**

Breeze approached after the 'party' started, and in **a shy way,** asked: "Do you know how to dance?"

"Not really. I, uh . . . I never really had the time."

'**Me neither.** Maybe we can learn together?"

"That **sounds like fun.** Sure. We'll have to do that someday."

"Why not **now**?"

> I was zapped by lightning again.
> Dance?! Right now?!
> I don't know how to dance!

Thankfully, the mobs—being the **gentlemobs** they are—must have sensed my embarrassment, and saved me in the nick of time. A **huge** army of zombies rushed out of that forest. **Of course,** they were all wearing helmets—like the "helmet squad" Kolbert had seen earlier. Here's where our plans fell apart.

You see, due to school safety regulations, only a few kids had **flint and steel** on them at the time.

Bumbi was one of them, along with Bubbles and Loaf—the teachers gave the flint and steel to these noobs so they had something to do. They were some of the super noobs behind those **Building Fails.** No one wanted them **building**—and who knows how they'd manage to mess up placing TNT.

Okay, so—those kids **ran.** They saw that huge army approaching, the helmets gleaming in the sun, and totally **chickened out.** So the rest of us couldn't light the TNT.

So we had
to retreat.

We had to go back **near the real village** and watch helplessly as the mobs began **dismantling Super Happy Fun Town.** The zombies trashed the jukeboxes first, which were all blaring loudly with annoying music. Then they went for the cakes, the pink glass, the seastone lanterns . . .

It looked like Lola's idea was **about to fail.**

Then her voice rang out like a note block set to a high pitch. "Looks like you guys didn't read the **instructions** very well! **But don't worry!** I expected this, so I did the last part myself!"

She was standing at the edge of the crowd, **next to a lever** that had been placed on the ground.

Also next to the lever, forming a long trail across the plains . . .
redstone dust.

We thought she was the ultimate noob . . .

She didn't think like us, she didn't act like us, she didn't speak like us . . .

But she was
hiding strength that
no one else had . . .

I judged her just like
Pebble had judged me. And
at that moment, I knew . . .

. . . I, too,
was wrong.

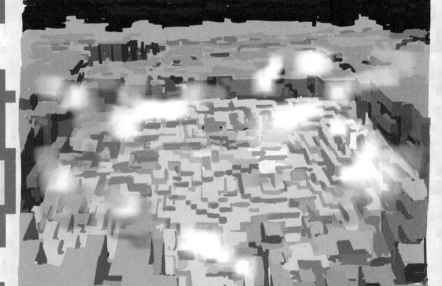

After the explosion, you couldn't see a single block of **Super Happy Fun Town** . . . and there **wasn't a mob in sight.** Since Lola had come up with this idea and was the one who'd laid **the redstone trail**—single-handedly obliterating over **three hundred zombies**—and since she was on **our team** . . .

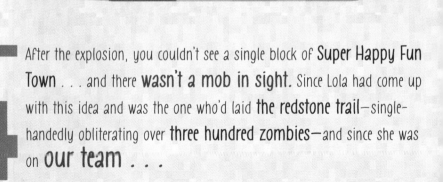

OPERATION SNOOP:
REPORT

OPHELIA	137
BREEZE	129
COGBOGGLE	128
RUNT	126
EMERALD	125
BLOCK	124
SOULSAND	122
PORCUPINE	120
TWINKLE	118
MAX	117

The crater also formed a kind of
no-mob's-land
between our village and the forest.

Man, those explosions were **legendary.** And here I thought we were going to use flint and steel! We were lucky those noobs **ran!**

The **first wave** of explosions knocked unlit TNT **in every direction.** If someone had lit them by hand, they would have been caught in the **blast area** . . .

It might require planning and lengthy setup time, but redstone does have combat applications. Can I stop being wrong about everything? Please?

I made good decisions from the beginning.

The wrong choice would have been to throw her off the team before the final exam.

***

The right choice was to believe in her, just like my friends and family believed in me.

If I'd chosen to not save Pebble, he'd definitely be a zombie.

There's still one decision left for me to make.

Despite all of the options, I felt like I had only one choice.

A **long time** ago, I started this diary with a single goal in mind. At the time, it seemed so **impossible,** so unattainable. **A ridiculous little dream.** I was barely a **full-size** villager then, who only knew about gathering seeds and planting crops. Now there's **a diamond pin on my cloak** and a diamond path just up ahead.

Am I **dreaming? Is this real?** I'm so caught up in this, I can barely write. Once more, I'm resisting the urge to create **tear blocks.** However, at the same time, it . . . feels like there is so much more waiting for me.

What about the **humans?** How did they arrive here? How will they **go back?** Are there more of them out there?

Then there are those weird dreams. Who is **Batwing? Clyde? Eeebs?** Is that cat **really a monster?** Do good monsters really exist? Above all else, there's a **man with glowing white eyes.** Is it possible that villagers, humans, and good monsters can work together to **stop him?**

Although the future seems so uncertain right now, I do know one thing for sure.

No matter what happens, **we'll keep fighting.** Somehow, some way, we'll **figure it all out.**

Before long, we will go out there, to a place once filled with people, from villagers to pigmen. Beyond our walls rests the knowledge the ancients left behind, which we must now **reclaim. With this knowledge,** we can craft obsidian swords, advanced redstone machines, enchanted arrows, powder kegs, and armor strong enough to withstand the strongest monsters—monsters thought to exist only in **fairy tales** and ancient times, which now haunt the Overworld **once more.**

The powder keg.

This morning, Breeze **asked me to go to the park.** After we sat under a tree, I figured we would craft food and have a **picnic** under the leaves. She pulled out **a diamond sword** instead.

"We **pooled our emeralds** together," she said, offering me the blade. "Even the mayor chipped in."

". . ."

In the sun, the blade had **a slight opalescent sheen,** so faint. Like Breeze, there was something **fragile** about its appearance, **elegant** and **graceful, beautiful.** Yet at the same time, it seemed strong enough to put up with a noob like myself *(also like Breeze).*

"I'm sorry if it seemed like I was **ignoring you,**" I said. "I didn't mean to hang out with Lola so much. I . . . just wanted us **to win.**"

"**It's my fault,**" she said. "When I saw you two spending so much time together, I couldn't control myself. **I was so jealous.** She's so talented in areas most villagers aren't."

"And you **aren't?**"

"No."

"Try telling that to pretty much every monster you've come across."

She smiled, but it **quickly faded.** "I'll . . . tell you **a secret.** Yesterday, when I stood before that chest, I . . . almost didn't **pull out a sword.**"

236

"What? Why?"

"I thought about **becoming a farmer**," she said. "I seriously considered it."

"I don't understand."

"**I'm tired of fighting,** Runt. It's all I've known. I just want a **peaceful** life, you know? Sunshine. Golden wheat fields. The smell of bread fresh off the crafting table."

"Maybe it's **not too late** to go back. Maybe the mayor will let you choose again."

She shook her head. "**I can't.** Even if I could, I wouldn't. Until this war is over, we'll never have any peace. And besides, there's another reason why I choose the sword."

"What?"

·You.·

(Okay, okay! We did hold hands this time! We did! I admit it!)

·Come on!·
she said, a few minutes later.
·We'll miss the celebration!
I'd really like to try dancing!·

"We're going to the hairdresser. We can't go to the party like this! **See ya later, Runt!**"

"Did you learn something about rune chambers? If you've made one, put me inside. I'm going to need to be enchanted with Whiner Protection VII!"

"The guards on the wall say they saw a villager outside, and the description sounds like Urf. I wonder if he'll be paying a visit sometime soon . . ."

"Yeaaaaaaah! I'm a captain, too! The Overworld dungeons are mine!"

"Good work, villagers!
I trained my men as well!
We'll work together to defeat
this son-of-a-noob Herobrine!"

"And actually, I saw Emerald
leave with Breeze and that redstone girl.
Where'd they go? And why am I always
thinking about her?"

This time, we deserved **a real celebration.** This time, we really did sing and laugh and dance, **even cry,** for we had to say good-bye—to the teachers, the classrooms, and all the times we had as innocent, carefree noobs.

All of which I already miss.

Breeze tapped me on the shoulder. She'd returned from the **salon** with Lola and Emerald.

Now she wore **a sleeveless robe,** and her hair had **the same kind of shimmer** as Lola's.

I'd heard about the salon. It's this place where you can **modify your skin or appearance.** Some of the human girls built it. I'll have to head over there at some point, because I heard you can **customize the appearance of your weapons and armor,** too.

If I really want to become OverlordRunt77777,
I'll have to look the part.

"This is called **a dress,**" she said. She whirled around. "Lola crafted it for me. And **the hair,** well . . . Elisa helped me do that."

"What about those things on your feet?"

"Slippers." She glanced down at herself. "So what do you think?"

"**You look amazing,**" I said. "I take back everything I said about human fashion." I paused. "Sure is changing around here, huh . . . ?"

"Yes, **our village is changing** . . . but that's not **a bad thing.**"

"Maybe not."

And suddenly I realized she'd said **our village.** She'd said it so **casually,** without any hesitation, as if she'd lived here all her life. She grabbed my hands and looked into my eyes, and in that moment I sensed that, at last, she was **truly home.**

"Our old way of life is **disappearing,**" she said. "We have to accept that, and look to the future. With the humans helping us, **we can win this war.** But let's forget about all that for today. Just today."

And her smile
was like an enchanted diamond.

"For today, we dance!"

PREVIOUS BOOKS

Diary of an 8-Bit Warrior

Diary of an 8-Bit Warrior: From Seeds to Swords

Diary of an 8-Bit Warrior: Crafting Alliances

Cube Kid is the pen name of Erik Gunnar Taylor, a writer who has lived in Alaska his whole life. A big fan of video games—especially Minecraft—he discovered early that he also had a passion for writing fan fiction.

Cube Kid's unofficial Minecraft fan fiction series, *Diary of a Wimpy Villager*, came out as e-books in 2015 and immediately met with great success in the Minecraft community. They were published in France by 404 éditions in paperback with illustrations by Saboten and now return in this same format to Cube Kid's native country under the title *Diary of an 8-Bit Warrior*.

When not writing, Cube Kid likes to travel, putter with his car, devour fan fiction, and play his favorite video game.